The
Runaways

OTHER YEARLING BOOKS BY ZILPHA KEATLEY SNYDER:

YEARLING BOOKS are designed especially to entertain and enlighten young people. Patricia Reilly Giff, consultant to this series, received her bachelor's degree from Marymount College and a master's degree in history from St. John's University. She holds a Professional Diploma in Reading and a Doctorate of Humane Letters from Hofstra University. She was a teacher and reading consultant for many years, and is the author of numerous books for young readers.

The
Runaways

ZILPHA KEATLEY SNYDER

A YEARLING BOOK

Fans can visit Zilpha Keatley Snyder's Web site! www.microweb.com/lsnyder/
Visit us on the Web! www.randomhouse.com/kids
Educators and librarians, for a variety of teaching tools, visit us at
www.randomhouse.com/teachers

ISBN: 0-440-41512-8

Reprinted by arrangement with Delacorte Press

Printed in the United States of America

August 2000

10 9 8 7 6 5 4 3 2 1

OPM

To Libby—who was there too

The
Runaways

chapter

1

Dani had been in the graveyard for maybe ten minutes when she suddenly knew she was going to do it. Jumping to her feet, she shook both fists in the air and yelled out loud, "Yeah, I'm going to." Took a deep breath and shouted again, "I really mean it."

It was like a vow, or maybe even more like—a challenge. Yeah. A challenge. Still staring up at the desert sky, she stuck out her chin and told herself, and anyone—or anything—that might be listening, that this time she absolutely meant it. She wasn't yelling now. Only thinking, but with a fierceness that swelled her throat as if she were still shouting, "I mean it. I'm going to do it. And right now, too."

No more of this waiting to grow up stuff, or even putting it off until next year. Any day now, like maybe next Friday, she,

Danielle O'Donnell, would load up her old purple duffel bag, take whatever money was left in Stormy's ugly bank and take off. On the bus if there was enough money for a ticket, or if that didn't work, by stowing away in the back of a truck. But however she had to do it, she was definitely going to go.

Afterward she never was quite sure why she'd made up her mind at that particular moment. It must have been the grave-yard that made the difference, that gave her the guts to finally come to a decision on an otherwise ordinary afternoon, the last day of April in 1951, a few months before her thirteenth birthday. It wasn't as if she'd been especially angry at that particular moment, or even any more bored out of her skull than usual. And for once the weather wasn't even especially awful. Okay, so the usual skin-shriveling desert wind was blowing, but at least it wasn't either icy cold or hot enough to broil your tonsils. So why did she suddenly make up her mind to do something she'd been putting off ever since she'd first set eyes on Rattler Springs more than four years ago? It must have been the graveyard that did it. Or else what she'd been doing there.

The graveyard at Rattler Springs was on a hill. Not much more than a slope really, but about the closest thing to a hill anywhere near town, and high enough so that from where she sat there was almost what you might call a view. You might, that is, if you'd grown up in Rattler Springs, and had never seen anything like a real one. A real view with lots of cool blue water, towering green trees and all the other great stuff Dan-ielle O'Donnell had been used to, once upon a time.

The "view" you actually got from the graveyard was of a

short row of squatty, sand-blistered shops, clustered around the only two-story building in town. That one big ugly building held a general store, a lunch counter, a small office and a big bar on the ground floor, and up above, the Grand Hotel. Or, as it was sometimes called, the Grablers' Grand. Everyone in town knew the Grablers, whether they wanted to or not.

Next door to the one big building there was the post office's little cubbyhole, about the size of a postage stamp, and on the other side of Main Street, a big wooden shack known as the town hall, which served as a church or movie theater, depending on the day of the week and time of day.

On past the town hall you got Lefty's Bar, one of the five bars in town, and right after that, the winner of any ugly contest, grubby old Gus's garage and service station. Gus's Grease Pit, as the whole place was sometimes called, consisted of a paintless gas station out front and, behind that, a big tin-roofed garage with its famous grease pit. The grease pit was famous, at least in Rattler Springs, because it was so deep, deeper than most grease pits because Gus was so tall. And greasier than most, because Gus was such a slob. And everywhere, in front, out back, in the garage and out of it, there were old tires, parts of dead cars and all kinds of other junk. And grease. Grease everywhere, especially on Gus himself.

Beyond the Grabler property and Greasy Gus's the town went on for about a block, but except for the Silver Grill, the only halfway decent restaurant in town, there wasn't much worth mentioning. The rest of Rattler Springs included a combination motel and gas station, a few more bars, and a scattering of houses and house trailers, spread out between

3

a lot of trashy vacant lots, with here and there a spindly, wind-stripped thing that never quite managed to look like a tree. Of course, there was also the schoolhouse, but that was another story. A story that didn't do much to improve Dani's feelings about the view.

It wasn't much of a school really, only two classrooms with a dark, narrow hallway between them. Dani had been in the primary room her first year at Rattler Springs. Since then she'd moved across the hall where Mr. Graham taught eighteen kids ranging in size from skinny little Chloe in the fifth grade to gigantic old Ronnie Grabler in the eighth. And not a person of any size who had any interest in anything outside of Rattler Springs.

Beyond and behind and around all of it was absolutely nothing. Nothing, that is, but desert. And not even an honest-to-God, Sahara-type desert like you see in pictures, where bare white dunes move in the wind like snowdrifts, and actually manage to look beautiful in a deadly sort of way. Nothing as interesting as that. Around Rattler Springs all you got was boring, gray-brown, flat-out ugliness, where the few things that did manage to grow were spindly or prickly, and not even big enough to hide behind. And in the distance the hills rose dark and slick against a bare, blue sky.

But it couldn't have been looking at the Rattler Springs view, as miserable as it was, that made Dani come to a decision. After all, she'd looked out across that same depressing scene plenty of times before. What really must have done it—and she realized that this was pretty freaky, but it was true—

what must have done it was seeing her own name on the tombstone. Even though she'd put it there herself.

She'd been sitting there on a flattish rock between the graves of Clarence Bailey and Hank Somebody-or-other when it happened. On her right was Clarence's tombstone, which she'd noticed before because it was the only one in the whole graveyard that was actually made of stone. Poor little dearly beloved Clarence Bailey. You knew he was little because he was born in 1891 and died in 1893. Which might seem like a sad story if you didn't stop to think that at least he'd escaped having to grow up in Rattler Springs. And you knew he was dearly beloved because somebody had gone to the trouble to put up a marble tombstone, instead of a wooden cross. Or even just a slab of wood, like the one over poor old illegible Hank.

The sad news on Clarence's marble tombstone was easy enough to read, but Hank's statistics were another matter. The writing on Hank's grave marker had been burned into the wood, probably with a branding iron. The first four letters were *H A N K,* she was fairly sure about that. But then came a last name that started with what might have been an *S,* before it faded away into a bunch of splinters. There was, in fact, only one spot on the weathered old slab that was still fairly smooth and it was there that Dani, for some unknown reason, had started to write her own name. Not branding it into the wood, like they'd done for poor old Hank, but only scratching it in with a rusty nail.

Danielle O'Don—she'd written, and then she'd stopped.

Stopped scratching and for a moment almost stopped breathing, with the horror of it. The horror of a terrible heart-stopping fear. It didn't come from the notion that she was going to die someday. She'd never wasted much energy worrying about that. But more likely from suddenly facing the possibility that she might die right there. That she might live out her whole life in Rattler Springs without ever escaping back to where she belonged.

It was then that she caught her breath, dropped the nail as if it had burned her fingers, jumped to her feet and started yelling. And then hushed, and stood motionless, only moving her eyes from one side to the other as she waited—and listened.

There was no answer, of course, at least not one that she heard with her ears, but the desert was talking to her, all right. Telling her that it wouldn't ever let her get away. Like it had almost every day for the last four years. Ever since that blazing hot day in 1947 when she and Linda had arrived in Rattler Springs. Dani shook her head fiercely, took a deep breath and began to run. But she'd only gone a few steps when she stumbled on a rock and turned her ankle.

It hurt. For a minute or two it hurt like anything. She hopped for a while, muttering "Ouch" and a few other things, before she managed to go on. Refusing to limp, she tried not to wonder if the desert had done it on purpose. Had put that rock there to let her know how easy it would be to stop her if she ever tried anything desperate. Showing her how it could use a sneaky rock, or the blazing sun, or just hundreds of miles of emptiness, to keep her from making it. "Nice try," she told the desert, "but you don't scare me any." She kept right on then at a slightly painful jog until she got to the end of the graveyard trail. And just beyond the trail's end, Silver Avenue.

chapter

2

Silver Avenue. Slowing to a walk and not even bothering to look both ways, Dani started right up the middle of the crumbling, potholed stretch of blacktop that some long-ago dreamer had the nerve to name Silver Avenue. "Sssil-ver Ah-ven-ooo." Dani always stuck out her chin and waggled her head around in a "grand lady" put-on, whenever she had to give her address. "Number seventeen, Sssil-ver Ah-ven-ooo." What a laugh. As if there had ever been much silver, or anything halfway grand enough to be called an avenue, in Rattler Springs.

She was almost home, still waggling her head and murmuring "Sss-il-ver" when, right behind her and practically in her ear, a voice said, "You going nuts or something?" Dani whirled around, but of course it was only Stormy.

"Nuts? Not me," Dani said. "But I will be if you don't stop sneaking up on me like that." Grabbing Stormy by his collar, she hissed in his ear, "Don't you know you can drive people crazy, doing stuff like that?"

She turned him loose then and, putting her hands on her hips, glared at him. Poor old Stormy Arigotti had been following her around like a pet dog ever since he'd come to Rattler Springs at least two years before. He'd moved right into the Grand Hotel because his mother worked there, and since Dani lived next door it hadn't taken Stormy long to start moving in on her. And not only when she was at home either. Stormy had a talent for showing up almost anywhere. Like in the middle of Silver Avenue, for instance.

She never had been able to figure out how a short, clunky nine-year-old kid could be so good at sneaking around. You'd be walking along, on your way to the rest room at school, or crossing the highway or even heading out to the trash can in your own backyard, for heaven's sake, and there he'd be, sudden and silent as a snake.

"Okay, what's up?" Dani asked him impatiently. "What do you want now?"

"Nothin'. Not exactly right now anyways, but . . ." Looking down sheepishly, Stormy began to pull something out of his jacket pocket. "But maybe later . . ."

It was a book, of course. Dani jerked it away from him. "What is it this time?"

"It's a short one," Stormy said. "See, it's just . . ." He reached out, trying to turn the book to the last page, but she snatched it away and put it behind her back. Stormy made a grab for it but she turned quickly, making him miss.

The book was called *White Fang* and the picture on the cover was of a wolfish-looking dog. It looked kind of interesting. At least a little bit better than some of the stuff Stormy brought her. Dani sighed. The trouble with Stormy was that he had a problem. Well, actually, a couple of problems that didn't fit together worth a darn. On the one hand, he had this reading block. Like when Stormy looked at a word the letters got all mixed up so what he saw didn't make much sense. But on the other hand he had this mad love affair with stories. Particularly stories about animals. Most of the time Stormy was a really active-type kid. He could run around for hours playing a stupid ball game, or chasing somebody who'd called him a bad name. But if someone was reading a story he'd do a complete personality switch. Listening to a story, Stormy Arigotti could sit still for so long you'd think he'd been turned to stone. You might, at least, if you didn't notice his eyes. When Stormy was listening to a story there was something about his eyes that always reminded Dani of the sparklers kids play with on the Fourth of July.

When Stormy lunged at the book again, she held it up over her head, grinning at him teasingly. She was thinking about telling him to forget it. After all, if she was going to be running away in a few days, she was going to be too busy getting ready to sit around for hours reading out loud. She was still keeping the book away from him when she saw his face tighten with anger and she got ready, watching his fists, but most of all his feet. Stormy was a mean kicker when he got mad enough, and she had the scars on her shinbones to prove it. He was almost kicking mad, one more teasing grin would probably have done it, when Dani decided to cool it.

Handing the book back to him, she said, "Okay, here it is. And I'll read it. But not now. After dinner. Okay?"

"Okay. After dinner." Stormy's snub-nosed face split into a jack-o'-lantern grin. "I'll bring pretzels. Okay? Or Beer Nuts?"

"Okay, okay," Dani muttered, and started on across the street to the historic old Jerky Joe cabin, where she and her mother had lived since right after they arrived in Rattler Springs. As usual, the sagging gate refused to open. Shoving and kicking it, she growled, "Grrreat. Just great."

Right behind her Stormy was bouncing around like a clown on a pogo stick. "Which?" he kept saying. "Which?"

One more violent kick and Dani gave up on the gate and whirled to face him. "Which what?" she bellowed.

Sounding hurt and startled, Stormy whispered, "Pretzels or Beer Nuts?"

Dani stopped to think. She liked them both, but you could buy pretzels at the store and the only place in Rattler Springs where you could get Beer Nuts was on the counter at the Grand Hotel bar—where no juveniles were allowed. No juveniles, at least, except someone whose mother worked at the bar and looked the other way while her kid snuck in to snitch Beer Nuts.

"Okay, Beer Nuts," she said. She watched Stormy clump happily off clutching his precious book and wondered how much money there'd be in her running-away fund if she had a nickel for every book she'd ever read to Stormy. Giving the stupid gate a final kick, she gave up and, walking down to the hole in the fence, she cut across the pitiful remains of a lawn and up the front steps and banged open the screen door. As she crossed the tiny combination living room–bedroom a voice called, "Dani. Is that you?"

The voice belonged, of course, to Dani's mother, Linda, who at the moment was sitting at the kitchen table with a cup of tea and a book.

"There you are," she said as Dani entered the room. "I was beginning to wonder."

"Oh yeah?" Dani asked. It crossed her mind to say that she was surprised to hear that a certain person had pulled her nose out of her book long enough to notice that her one and only kid was missing. But she didn't. Instead she went to the sink, rummaged around for a halfway clean glass, ran some luke-warm water and drank it, looking over the rim at her mother.

Linda O'Donnell was a pale, wispy woman who might have been almost pretty if she'd halfway tried. Tried to dress in something modern, for instance, instead of the long, saggy, flowery things she usually wore. And if she'd comb her fly-away hair once in a while and put on a little lipstick, which she might have time to do if she didn't waste so much time listening to soap operas on the radio. Not to mention reading dumb books about rich people, or else about poor girls who wind up marrying rich people and living happily ever after.

"What is it this time?" Dani asked, and when Linda turned the book to its front cover Dani couldn't help grinning. *The Pirate's Bride,*" she read in a dramatic voice. "Wowee!"

Linda smiled sheepishly, saved her place with a bookmark

and closed the book. The bookmark was an embarrassing old thing that Dani had made for her a long time ago. It was decorated with pictures of daisies along with some flowery print that said "I love to read." Dani had made it before she started noticing how her mother wasted so much time reading instead of doing something useful, like—Dani put her glass back down on the cluttered sinkboard—like washing a few dishes now and then, for instance.

After Linda closed her book and started making dinner Dani plopped herself down in her mother's chair and began to flip through *The Pirate's Bride*. It looked boring, like most of the stuff her mother read. Just a bunch of mushy stuff about a handsome man who acts mean and dangerous at first and then turns out to be positively adorable, and a beautiful woman who doesn't know she's in love with him even though it's perfectly obvious. Dani hated the books her mother read. And she hated the way her mother spent so much time reading and daydreaming instead of doing something about the mess they were in. Or at least worrying about it.

Linda said she didn't worry much because she was a natural optimist, which meant that she really believed in happy endings. Happy endings as in finding a better job so she could pay off their debts and save up enough money so she and Dani could leave Rattler Springs forever and move back to Sea Grove. But in the meantime she only sat around reading books like *The Pirate's Bride*. Dani slammed the book shut and shoved it away from her.

Her mother, who had started peeling things at the sink, looked back over her shoulder.

"What's the matter, Dani?" she asked.

Dani shrugged. She couldn't very well tell her mother that she was feeling a little nervous and jumpy because she was about to run away. But she could talk about the stupid book. "I don't know," she said. "It's just that I don't see how you can waste so much time reading stuff like that instead of doing something to . . ." She took a deep breath and then went on, "to get us back to Sea Grove."

Linda sighed. She came back to the table, bringing the carrot she was peeling. Sitting down at the table, she peeled another long strip and then just sat there, staring at Dani. Not an angry stare. Dani wished it were. She could be angry too then, and not feel guilty about it. Finally Linda said, "Like what? Just what do you see me doing that might change things?"

"Well, like . . . like . . . ," Dani began, and then stammered to a stop. Her mother was smiling at her in the pitiful way that always drove Dani crazy. "Well, in the first place you might . . . Well, in the first place we never should have left Sea Grove. That's what's in the very first place." Then she went into her bedroom and threw herself down on the bed.

chapter
3

That much was the truth for sure. If only Linda hadn't quit her job and given up the lease on their Sea Grove house before she'd even seen Rattler Springs.

The house in Sea Grove. Even after four years Dani could close her eyes and see exactly how it had looked. It hadn't been very big, that was for sure, and maybe it was a little bit shabby in an artistic sort of way. But it was on a hillside, beside a grove of incredibly tall redwood trees, and from one end of the front porch there was this incredible view of the ocean. And the school where Dani had gone ever since kindergarten was only about a mile away. A school where she liked everybody and nearly everybody liked her, instead of hating her just because she was new and different. And where

Heather Brady, her best friend, lived just down the road with her big, friendly family.

Dani had only been eight years old when they'd left for Rattler Springs, but she'd known right away it was a bad idea. Even right at first when everybody thought that Linda had inherited a real ranch, like something out of a Roy Rogers movie. The whole inheritance thing had happened because Chance Gridley, who had been Linda's husband for a while when Dani was around five or six years old, had always had a dream about being a big-time cattle rancher.

Actually Dani had some pretty good memories of Chance. For one thing she remembered what a good storyteller he'd been. But according to Linda, it turned out that she and Chance didn't have very much in common, and besides he had this little problem with drinking and gambling. Like going to Reno and gambling away all his money so they had nothing to live on but Linda's salary. So there was a divorce and Dani's mother went back to being Linda O'Donnell. And Chance went off to live in Nevada. He must have gone right on gambling because all at once some kind of miracle happened and he won a whole bunch of money. Enough money anyway to buy a lot of land. At least that was what his letters to Linda began to tell about.

It had been a more or less friendly divorce, and every once in a while Chance would write back to Linda and Dani and tell them how much he still loved both of them, and about the huge cattle ranch he owned now. A cattle ranch near what he said was a nice little Western town called Rattler Springs. And every once in a while he'd send Linda a little child support money even though he didn't have to, because Dani's real father had died in the war before Chance and Linda had even met. So Linda would write back to thank him and tell him how she and Dani were getting along.

And then one day they'd gotten a letter from a lawyer saying that Chance had died of a heart attack, and that he'd left more than a thousand acres and a big old ranch house to Linda and Dani. And it just so happened that right at that time Linda was in the middle of her Western romances period, reading lots of books by people like Zane Grey and Louis L'Amour. Dani remembered that when Linda began to talk about moving she'd made it sound as if the ranch were in a big green valley with all kinds of barns and corrals scattered around, and horses and cattle and handsome cowboys everywhere you happened to look. And then, without even waiting to see the ranch first, she sold their car and bought an old wreck of a truck, packed everything they owned into it, and they took off. And it hadn't been until they'd gotten to Rattler Springs that they'd found out the awful truth.

The truth about Rattler Springs was that there'd never been much ranching in the area because there just wasn't enough water or grass. And the truth about the ranch house was that even though it was big and kind of interesting in some ways, it didn't have electricity or an indoor toilet. And it was about six miles from town, which was a big problem because Linda's old truck had broken down for good by then, and there wasn't enough money left to buy even a cheap old car. Nobody could live six miles from Rattler Springs without a car, so they'd only stayed a few days on their so-called ranch. And when

Linda had finally given up and decided to sell the ranch and move back to Sea Grove, she'd found that nobody wanted to buy their worthless, dried-out land. Not even if she practically gave it away. So Linda had found a lousy job in town, and they'd rented the so-called Jerky Joe cabin, and they'd been there ever since. Linda kept saying that they'd move back home as soon as she'd saved up a little money, but four years had gone by and she never saved anything. Instead she read and daydreamed and got more and more into debt, and the desert kept right on telling Dani how it had her now and she was never going to get away.

"Only not for much longer." Dani rolled over onto her stomach and smashed her fist into the pillow. "You hear me? I won't be here much longer." She got up then and started rummaging around in her closet looking for the duffel bag she'd had ever since they'd left Sea Grove. When she found it she dusted it off, opened it up and dumped it out on her bed.

There wasn't much in the bag. Just a few almost forgotten toys. Little-kid stuff she'd insisted on bringing to Rattler Springs and then had almost immediately outgrown. Things like a small, bristly teddy bear, a Raggedy Ann doll and a homemade stuffed toy that kind of resembled a deformed elephant. After emptying out all the junk Dani climbed up and got her hideous pig bank off the high shelf where she always kept it.

The bank had been a present from Stormy. He'd won it at the school fair almost two years before and he'd insisted on giving it to Dani. Sitting back down on the bed, Dani held the bank in both hands and studied it carefully. It was made out of very heavy pottery and it was supposed to look like some kind of wild boar. Its enormous snout was covered with warts, there was a ridge running down its back and big fangs jutted out of its lower lip. Actually it was kind of artistic looking, in a disgusting sort of way. Dani shook it, trying to guess how much money was inside. If there might be, for instance, anywhere near enough for a one-way ticket to the coast of northern California with transfers in Reno and San Francisco.

It was hard to tell. The pig did feel pretty heavy, and she could remember putting quite a lot of money into it, on her birthdays and Christmas and when she earned a little by baby-sitting or helping out at the bookstore. But she also remembered shaking some out now and then when something urgent came up, like a new inner tube for her bicycle. She kind of hated to break the ugly old bank but she knew from experience that you could only get the small coins out by shaking. This time several minutes of shaking only produced a dime or two and three nickels. Not even a glimpse of the bills or silver dollars that she knew were in there. So after a while she gave up and went out to find a hammer.

When she got back to her room, she put the wild boar bank in the middle of her bed and stood over it, telling herself that it was a hideous thing anyway and she'd always hated it. "Okay, pig, this is it," she whispered, and closing her eyes, she gave it a hard whack. But when she opened them there it was, still pretty much in one piece except for a broken front leg. She raised the hammer and was getting ready to try again when she heard her mother calling her to dinner.

Suddenly realizing how hungry she was, she threw the hammer down beside the bank and headed for the kitchen. Dinner that night was quiet and boring. It was boring because the food was mostly boring leftovers, and it was quiet because—well, because Dani didn't feel much like talking. Linda chattered away as usual, though, about the weather and what was happening to the people in her favorite soap operas, and then about what had happened at the bookstore that day.

The bookstore, or Cooley's Book Rental, was in a little building next to the Rattlesnake Bar and just across the street from the Grand Hotel. Actually it was a sort of cross between a bookstore and a library without really being either one. Some of the books were for sale and some could be rented for ten cents a day, but they were mostly secondhand and pretty beat-up looking. And old Al Cooley, who owned the store, was as old and worn out as his books. Which was a good thing actually because just about the time Dani and Linda arrived in town, Mr. Cooley decided he needed a helper and Linda got the job. Not much of a job really, but along with the little bit of money the government gave Dani because her father had died in the war, it was enough to keep two people more or less alive. But according to Linda, not nearly enough to move two people and all their belongings back home, where they'd have to rent a house and buy food to live on until Linda found another job.

Dani had just about finished her boring corned beef hash when Linda leaned over and said, "Dani. What is it? You're a thousand miles away tonight. What's on your mind?"

Actually, the "thousand miles away" stuff was kind of a

jolt. It was almost as if her mother had read her mind. Had guessed that she was planning on being, well, maybe not a thousand miles away but at least a few hundred, very soon now. Dani couldn't help feeling a little guilty as she said, "On my mind? Nothing much. I'm just . . . It's just that I told Stormy I'd read to him tonight, and I don't want to."

"Oh?" Linda tried to put the last of the hash on Dani's plate. "You don't want to? Why not?"

Dani pushed the spoon away. "Because. Because I've got other things to . . . And just because I hate it. I hate reading."

"Oh?"

Dani glared. She'd said she hated reading to make Linda angry, and all she'd gotten was that soft, wide-eyed, "Oh?" That, Dani told herself, was what she really hated. The way Linda always made "Oh" into a question.

"Well," Linda said, "it's too bad you hate it, because you're really exceptionally good at it, you know. I was listening to you the other night when you were reading *Doctor Dolittle* to Stormy and I was fascinated. You were changing your voice just a tiny bit for each of the animals, and you were every bit as good as that woman who reads on the radio. You know, the one who calls herself the Babbling Bookworm?"

Dani got up from the table very carefully and deliberately. She put her dish in the sink and then turned slowly around before she said, "Well, I *do* hate it. And what I *really* hate is when people sneak around listening to things they weren't invited to listen to." She was still standing there at the sink just waiting for Linda to do the "Oh?" thing, and thinking how she was going to hate that too, when without any warning the kitchen door crashed back against the wall. No sound of footsteps on the back porch, no knock on the door, no warning of any kind. Just *bang* as the door flew open, and there he was in the middle of the room, clutching his precious book in one hand and a greasy bag of Beer Nuts in the other.

Dani jumped, gulped and then glared. He'd done it again. Snuck up on her, and this time on her mother too. Linda was still clutching the bowl of hash. Her startled gaze turned into a smile. "Well, hello there, Stormy," she said. "Do come in."

chapter

4

"Hi." Stormy's grin almost split his face in two. "You guys finished eating?"

"Just about," Linda said. With the spoon still poised above the bowl, she turned to Dani. "You're sure you don't want the rest of this?"

Dani probably would have said no again, or she might not have, but before she could say anything at all Stormy said, "Hey. That looks good. I'll eat it." And then he did. Plopping himself down at the table, he began to eat right out of the serving bowl, shoveling the hash into his mouth at an incredible rate of speed. Over his head Linda caught Dani's eye and made a face that said something like "poor hungry kid." Dani shrugged. A person who was about to take off on a long, probably hungry, journey didn't have any sympathy left over for a kid who, at least, always had plenty of pretzels and Beer Nuts. Turning her back on the disgusting scene at the kitchen table, she headed for her room, but a second later Stormy was right behind her, stepping on her heels as he called back to her mother over his shoulder.

"Bye," he mumbled over the last mouthful of hash. "We're going to read now. Thanks for the . . . ?" He swallowed, poked Dani and whispered, "What was it?"

"Hash," Dani said.

"Oh yeah. Thanks for the hash."

As she opened the door of her room she could hear her mother telling Stormy that he was quite welcome. But at that moment Dani remembered what she'd left lying right out in plain sight in the middle of the bed. The broken-legged pig bank, and beside it—the hammer.

For a moment Stormy was too busy arranging Dani's beanbag chair to notice. Dani's chair, a huge canvas bag full of dry beans, could be shoved and punched into different shapes to fit the rear end of the person who was going to sit on it. Stormy always rearranged it violently before he sat down to listen to Dani read. So while he was still punching and shoving, Dani started to slide the pig bank quietly toward the head of the bed, where it could be hidden under a pillow. She'd almost made it when she heard a voice, a shocked, accusing voice, saying, "Why'd you do that? Why'd you break your bank?"

Trying to sound innocent, Dani said, "Break? Why'd I . . ." She picked up the pig's broken leg and put it back where it belonged, but of course it only fell off again. She was about to say that the bank must have fallen off the shelf when Stormy had banged the kitchen door open, when she noticed that Stormy's accusing gaze had moved to the hammer. He grabbed it up and went on staring, his eyes moving from the hammer to Dani and back again. Even more than usual, his round, flat face looked like a Halloween jack-o'-lantern. Only instead of a grinning jack-o'-lantern it was an openmouthed, owl-eyed one. He gulped once or twice and then his eyes narrowed to a suspicious squint. "You're going to run away, aren't you?" he said.

And then it was Dani's turn to feel shocked, because for a moment it seemed like Stormy had turned into some kind of a weird mind-reading wizard. How else could he know? After all, there were all sorts of things a person could need money for besides running away. He'd watched her shake money out of the bank before. How did he know she wasn't just going to buy another inner tube?

But then suddenly she remembered something she'd said almost two years before, when Stormy had given her the bank. Something she hadn't really meant, at least not at the time. But she'd just had an extra-bad day at school, and a quarrel with Linda, and the weather had been even more horrible than usual. So when Stormy insisted on giving her the bank as a bribe to get her to read *Tom Sawyer* over again, she'd told him it was the ugliest thing she'd ever seen, but she would keep it because it would be a perfect place to keep her running-away fund. It was the perfect place because it was so ugly that every time she looked at it, it would remind her of Rattler Springs, which would make her remember to save running-away money. So she got an ugly pottery pig out of the deal, and Stormy got the chance to hear every word of *Tom Sawyer* all over again, starting on page one.

The memory of exactly what she promised that day was just beginning to come back when Stormy said, "You said you wouldn't break it until you were ready to run away." He was really glaring now, his face tight as a clenched fist. "You said that. Didn't you?"

"Wellll." Dani stretched the word out, stalling while she tried to decide what to say next. Stalling at least until she noticed Stormy's face, and how he was holding the hammer in one hand, as if he might be getting ready to hit something, or somebody, with it. "Now wait a minute," she said. "I'm not really getting ready to run away. Not yet, anyway. I was just starting to make some plans."

The thundercloud face didn't lighten up. "Were you going to tell me? Were you going to tell me before you did it?"

Dani thought of saying, "No. Why should I tell you?" But instead she sighed and then said, "Yeah. Sure. I'd have told you before I left. Probably I would."

Stormy shook his head. "No," he said firmly. "No! Not probably. You *have* to tell me as soon as you start thinking about it because—because I'm going too. When you run away you have to take me with you."

That was too much. It was all Dani could do to keep from laughing. But she didn't laugh. She knew Stormy's quick temper well enough to know that to laugh at him while he was holding a hammer wasn't a particularly smart thing to do. So she controlled her twitching lips and said, "How could I take you with me?" She pointed at the bank. "There's probably not even enough money in there for one person's tickets, leave alone two. And besides, what about your mother? She'd have a fit."

"What about yours?"

"That's different."

"Different? No, it isn't. What's different about it?"

Dani didn't know if she could make Stormy understand but she decided to try. "Well, in the first place, I'm older."

Stormy's eyes got squintier. He always hated any mention of the fact that Dani was older than he was.

She went on hurriedly. "And in the second place, if I disappeared my mother would know why, and she'd probably guess I'd gone back to Sea Grove. So, if she was really worried, all she'd have to do is come after me. But if you disappeared your mother wouldn't know why, or where or anything. So she'd be a lot more apt to get hysterical."

Stormy only shook his head, glowering up at Dani from under his eyebrows and muttering something under his breath.

"Mutter, mutter, mom, mutter, mutter, care," it sounded like. Or possibly, "My stupid mom wouldn't even care." Dani thought of asking him if that was what he'd said, but on second thought . . . Everybody in Rattler Springs, at least everybody at Rattler Springs school, knew better than to say anything at all to Stormy about his mother. They knew because a few of them had tried it, and one of them had lost a front tooth. Stormy wasn't very big but he was tough and determined and where his mother was concerned he could get pretty violent. He'd slugged a boy once just for calling her Gorgeous Gloria, which was what everybody called her, at least when Stormy wasn't around. So Dani changed the subject to why. "Why on earth do *you* want to run away? I thought you said you liked Rattler Springs."

At first Stormy only shrugged and scowled, but at last he said, "I don't really *want* to. Not for good anyway. I just want to go along till you get there. Then I'll probably come back."

Dani couldn't help laughing. "That's crazy," she said. "You mean you just want to go along for the trip? Like a tourist or something?"

Stormy didn't laugh. "No!" he said loudly, and then more softly, "Yeah, maybe." His squinted eyes rounded a little. "Well, why not? What's so funny about that?"

"What's so funny?" She was laughing again. "Well, for one thing." She struggled to straighten out her face. "For one thing it's not going to be the kind of trip you go on for fun. It will probably be the kind where you might have to walk part of the way, or stow away in the back of a truck. And it might even be dangerous."

"Dangerous?" Stormy's eyes were really round now.

Dani nodded.

"Who . . . ? What . . . ? What kind of dangerous?"

"Oh, I don't know. Because of dangerous people, I guess. Like maybe people who pick you up when you're hitchhiking. Or just because it takes too long to get there and you run out of money and starve to death."

The starving bit was good, she thought. Anybody who liked to eat as much as Stormy did would be sure to hate the idea of starving. But to her surprise it only seemed to make him more stubborn than ever. "I'm going," he said. "If you go you *have* to take me too." He wasn't raving now or whispering. Just speaking in an ordinary dead calm voice. Dead calm and determined.

But Dani could be determined too. She shook her head and was still shaking it when Stormy said, "Promise. Promise I'm going too. If you don't I'll . . ."

"What? What will you do?"

Dani was still sitting on the edge of the bed with the broken pig bank in her lap, and Stormy was standing in front of her holding the hammer in both hands. Hands that were clenched so tightly the knuckles were turning white. Keeping the hammer in the edge of her vision, Dani asked cautiously, "What will you do if I don't promise?"

Stormy's face had turned back into an angry mask. "If you don't promise—I'll tell."

Dani couldn't believe it. Stormy Arigotti wasn't exactly perfect. She'd always known that he was a sneak and a shin kicker, for instance, not to mention a hyperactive nonreader. But it was hard to believe that he was actually threatening to snitch on her running-away plans. Sitting there silent and blank-eyed as a statue, Dani told herself she didn't believe it. But at the same time, her mind was racing around like crazy. Around and around, picking up ideas and then putting them down again.

First of all she thought of telling him what people thought of snitches. How snitches were just about the lowest of the low and . . . But then she realized that wouldn't help at all.

Stormy didn't care what people thought of him. Some of the time he didn't even care what Dani thought of him.

Then she had a great idea. At least for a moment, it seemed like a great idea. "If you do," she started, making every word count. "If-you-tell-I'll-never . . ." She stopped there. What she'd been planning to say was that she'd never read to him again. But, of course, that was pretty stupid because if he didn't tell, she would go ahead and run away, and there'd be no more reading anyway. Stormy might not have been the smartest kid in the world, but he was smart enough to figure that out.

Finally she gave up. At least she gave up on trying to come up with an argument that would convince Stormy to keep his mouth shut. And that only left letting him come too. Or—she thought for a moment longer—or at least letting him *think* he was going to come too. Putting one hand behind her back—the one with the crossed fingers—she said, "All right. I give up. I guess you can come with me."

"I can? You promise?"

Dani nodded.

Stormy lifted the hammer over his head. "Okay," he said. "Let's smash the pig."

chapter
5

The money in the pig bank turned out to be a big disappointment. It had felt so heavy that Dani was sure there would be at least fifty dollars, but it turned out to be only thirty-three dollars and seventeen cents. And that meant there wasn't anywhere near enough. Dani knew she'd have to transfer twice and by checking the bus schedule in the post office she'd discovered that the first leg of the journey, from Rattler Springs to Reno, would be thirteen dollars and fifty cents. At least that was what it was for an adult ticket, which meant anyone twelve years old or older. The trouble was, she wasn't sure exactly how much the ticket on to San Francisco and then the one to Sea Grove would be. And she didn't dare ask anybody for fear of giving away her plans. But as near as she'd been able to figure, the tickets to go all the way to Sea Grove by bus would be almost forty dollars. And that was just for one person. Of course Stormy could buy a child's ticket, but that would only be a few dollars less.

"For two of us," she told Stormy, "we're going to need almost eighty dollars and that's not even counting money for stuff to eat."

Stormy said that was all right because he could bring lots of Beer Nuts, and then he insisted on counting the money all over again. He was much better at counting than reading, particularly money counting, but when he'd finished the results were just the same. Thirty-three dollars and seventeen cents.

"Not enough," Stormy said gloomily.

Dani shrugged. "Nowhere near." Then, slanting a sideways look at him, she started to say, "Well, too bad. I guess you'll have to stay—"

"No," Stormy interrupted. "No I won't. We'll both have to wait till we get some more money."

Shaking her head fiercely, Dani said, "No. No, I can't wait. I have to go. I have to get out of here."

"Why?"

Dani glared. "Why?" She took a deep breath. "I'll tell you why." And then she began to do something she'd never done before. To tell Stormy something she'd never told anyone in the whole world. All about that day back in 1947 when she was only eight years old and she and Linda had arrived in Rattler Springs on a scorching summer day. How they had climbed out of their ancient truck into the ugly nothingness and lung-scorching heat of Rattler Springs. "And it was right then," she told him, "that very first day, that I began to hear the desert telling me I'd have to stay forever. I could hear it plain as day. Not with my ears really, but sort of inside my head. And I still hear it. Not all the time. Not so much when I'm indoors, but almost any time when I'm outside. Whenever I look around at all the dry, dead . . ." She paused, waving her arms in a circle. ". . . or up at the sky. When I look up at the sky I can hear it almost every time. The sky is part of it, and the sun, and the wind too. It's like a lot of voices but all of them put together are the desert talking to me. And they're all saying the same thing."

Stormy had collapsed into the beanbag chair in his usual listening position, with his backside sunk into the deep dent he'd made in the middle of it and his arms and legs sprawling out in every direction. His usual twitchy movements had disappeared, and his eyes had gone wide and glittery. Now and then his head nodded slightly, the way it always did when . . .

Suddenly Dani saw what was happening. Stormy thought he was listening to a story. He was just sitting there dreaming along with what she was telling him, exactly as if she were reading *Tom Sawyer*, or some book of fairy tales. As if the whole thing about the desert and the way she felt about it and why she had to get away were all part of some kind of fairy story she'd been telling herself. Like Linda's daydream stories about princes or pirates or handsome cowboys who were going to come along someday and make everything wonderful. The thought made Dani very angry because . . . She didn't really know why it made her so angry, but she knew she was going to find out.

"Hey, you," she whispered so sharply that Stormy jumped and blinked. "Wake up. This isn't some dumb daydream. This is for real."

"For real?" Stormy's eyes were back to normal now. "What kind of for real?"

"Something that really happened. And real plans about what I have to do next."

"Plans?" Stormy asked. Then he scratched his head and let his eyes roll thoughtfully and very slowly from one side to the other. Which, as usual, made Dani want to shake him. "I don't get it," he said finally.

Between clenched teeth Dani said, "What don't you get?"

"I don't get the difference."

"What do you mean you don't get the difference?"

"The difference between plans and daydreams."

Dani shook her head in amazement. "You don't? You don't know the difference between plans and—"

But suddenly Stormy was pushing himself up out of the beanbag. "Hey," he said. "Listen. Somebody's knocking. Real loud."

Dani heard it too. Someone was pounding on the back door.

"Who is it?" Stormy asked, looking at Dani as if he thought she had X-ray vision or something.

Dani made her shrug say she didn't know and didn't care. But she was curious. Just to be safe she started gathering up the money from the pig bank and putting it in the top drawer of her dresser, and then scooping up the broken pieces of pig. She had just finished dumping the pig scraps into the wastepaper basket when there was a light rap on her bedroom door and Linda came in.

Linda was looking puzzled, Dani decided, and maybe a little bit pleased.

"What was that?" Stormy demanded. "Sounded like someone breaking the door down."

"It was Ronnie," Linda said, "with a message from some people who are staying at the hotel."

"Yeah." Dani rolled her eyes. "Should have known it was old Ronnie. Who else knocks like that?"

Ronnie was the fifteen-year-old son of the Grablers, who owned the General Store and Grand Hotel and Bar, as well as the land around it, which included the historic old Jerky Joe cabin where the O'Donnells lived. All of which, some people in town said, the Grablers had kind of stolen from Jerky Joe's descendants. So Linda knew the adult Grablers, Howie and Brenda, pretty well. Knew too much about them actually, like the fact that they were lousy landlords, raising the rent all the time and refusing to repair anything. And Dani knew a lot about Ronnie Grabler too. At the Rattler Springs school Ronnie was practically famous for pounding on anything that got in his way. Like doors, for instance, but also car fenders, and other people's belongings. Not to mention the faces of quite a few of his classmates. But right at the moment Dani couldn't think of any reason why Ronnie might be mad at her. Stormy seemed to be pretty much in the dark too.

"Was that all old Ronnie wanted?" Dani asked cautiously.

"I think so," Linda said. "All he said was that some people who are staying at the hotel want to talk to me." Linda looked at a piece of notebook paper. "Some people named Smithson?" She looked at Dani and Stormy questioningly as if she thought they might know who the Smithsons were. They both shook their heads.

"I'll just run over and see what's up," Dani's mother said. "You two go on reading. I'll be right back." Linda picked up Dani's hairbrush and gave her flyaway hair a whack or two before she went out.

Dani didn't expect her mother to be gone long since the hotel was only a few yards away, if you went in the handy back way through the lunchroom kitchen. While she was gone Stormy went back to the subject of how they could make some money for bus tickets. He even suggested some things they might try—like starting a car-washing business, or else maybe robbing a bank.

Dani pointed out that the car-washing idea might work anywhere else but in Rattler Springs where all the cars were so old and ugly that nobody bothered to wash them. And as for bank robbery, she thought he was kidding, but with Stormy it wasn't easy to tell. She was thinking of telling him that her bank-robbing license had just expired, when Linda returned. She had, she told them excitedly, wonderful news.

Dani wasn't too thrilled. Optimistic Linda was always dreaming up great things that were about to happen. Like the wonderful cattle ranch they were heading for when they left

Sea Grove, for instance. "What kind of wonderful news?" Dani asked suspiciously.

"Well, the Smithsons." Linda took a business card out of her pocket and studied it carefully. "Well, it seems that Ivor and Emily Smithson are geologists and they—"

"Are what?" Stormy interrupted. "What are ge—what you said—what are they?"

"Geologists are people who study the earth," Linda told him. "Rocks and minerals and things like that. Anyway, it seems the Smithsons are going to be doing some work in this area and they're staying at the hotel while they look for a place to rent. I guess someone told them about the ranch house and they thought it might be just what they're looking for." Linda smiled and blinked in a dazed sort of way. "They actually wanted to talk to me about the possibility of renting it for a few months."

"For sure?" Dani felt a little dazed herself. Dazed and astounded. "Did they say for sure?"

"Well, no. Not yet," Linda said. "They have to see it first, of course. But tomorrow they're going to pick me up and drive out to see if it suits them."

"They're going to pick you up tomorrow?"

Linda nodded. "Yes. According to the Grablers they have a very unusual car. Specially made for going over rough ground. Howie said it looks like a cross between a Cadillac and a Sherman tank. Custom built and very expensive, Howie says."

"And you think people who drive custom-built cars would want to live in our ranch house?" Dani asked in amazement.

Linda shook her head. "Doesn't seem possible, does it? But they seemed interested even after I told them all about it. Even about no electricity and all. And Howie Grabler said he heard them say they could go as high as seventy-five dollars a month."

Linda was looking very excited. Her cheeks weren't as pale as usual and her eyes had a kind of shine to them. Before she left the room she said, "Just think, Dani, how much that would help with the bills."

Dani thought about it, but she didn't get too excited. For one thing seventy-five dollars a month was an awful lot of rent to pay for a house that didn't even have electricity or an indoor toilet. Dani didn't know much about geologists but she had a feeling that they were probably pretty intelligent people. The kind who'd be too smart to pay seventy-five dollars a month for a place that didn't even have an indoor toilet.

After Linda had gone back to the kitchen Stormy said, "Hey, that's great about the seventy-five dollars, isn't it? Maybe your mom will let you have some of it for—"

"Oh sure," Dani interrupted him in her most sarcastic tone of voice. "Oh sure, just as soon as my mom starts getting some extra money she'll be glad to contribute to my running-away fund. As a matter of fact, I think I'll pass the hat or something." Dani paraded around the room pretending to be passing a hat. "Hi, folks," she said in a phony radio-commercial tone of voice. "How'd you like to contribute to my running-away—" She got about that far before Stormy charged.

Kicking and slugging, he yelled, "Shut up. Stop it. I didn't mean that. You know that's not what I meant."

Backed into a corner, Dani held him off with both hands, and watched while his angry face crumpled into misery. "That wasn't what I said," he kept saying. "I just meant she might give you an allowance or something and then you could—"

"Hey, I know. I know what you meant." She wouldn't tell Stormy she was sorry, but she was, at least a little. She knew how Stormy worried about being dumb and how he hated it when people teased him about saying dumb things. And actually what he'd said did make some sense when you stopped to think about it. Dani never had had an allowance but she supposed she might get one if Linda weren't so broke all the time. And an allowance *could* be spent for almost anything. Even bus tickets.

"Hey," she said. "We haven't read yet. Where's the new book?"

A few seconds later Stormy was back in the beanbag and Dani was beginning the first page of *White Fang*.

chapter

6

Dani didn't believe it when Linda said the geologists were going to pick her up and take her out to see the ranch house. Not for a minute. Lying in bed that night, Dani told herself that the whole thing was just another of Linda's hopelessly optimistic daydreams. There was absolutely no use waiting around indefinitely for rent money from the ranch house to provide an allowance. If she was going to escape it would have to be right away, even if she had to hitchhike or stow away in the back of a truck.

But the very next day Dani was in the living room when she noticed a strange purring noise that seemed to be coming from Silver Avenue. Getting on her knees on the daybed, she peered out through a rip in the ragged drapes, in time to see a strange-looking black vehicle pulling to a stop right in front of

the cabin. Built high off the ground, the black car-truck-tank
—whatever it was—had oversized wheels and huge fat tires.
There were carrying racks on the roof, and in front of the
racks there was a roundish thing that looked like some kind of
turret or fuel tank. She wouldn't have believed it if she hadn't
seen it with her own eyes. But she had. And not only the
weird car, but also the two fairly weird people who got out of
it.

The man looked tough and wiry, with bushy eyebrows that
jutted out over a long, narrow face, and the woman was small
and thin, with dark blond hair that she wore pulled back into
a ponytail. Even though they were wearing khaki trousers and
cotton shirts they had, Dani decided, a big-city look about
them. It had something to do with their slick, smooth features and the way they moved, like people who knew exactly
what they were doing, and why. Not many Rattler Springs
residents moved that way, particularly not on a sweltering
afternoon.

The strange couple were still fussing with the broken gate
when Linda hurried out wearing her best dress and newest
sandals. The three of them talked and shook hands, and when
the gate finally opened they all climbed into the car and it
crept off up Silver Avenue. Dani watched until it was out of
sight before she collapsed on the couch. She lay there for
quite a while imagining the embarrassing scene when those
slick, sophisticated city folks got a look at Linda's so-called
ranch.

Dani kept telling herself, just like she'd told Stormy the
night before, that she didn't have a hope in the world that

41

they would want to rent the place after they'd seen it. Oh, it was big and roomy, all right, at least compared to most Rattler Springs houses, but it never had been exactly a palace. And she could just imagine what it must look like now that it had been sitting there collecting dust for almost four years. Dani could picture the expressions on the faces of those city people when they checked out the dust, and the beat-up old kitchen with its rusty iron sink, and the outhouse toilet a few yards from the back door.

The big-wheeled black car didn't come back for a long time. When a couple of hours had gone by Dani began to worry. Who knew, she asked herself, what might happen when an unsuspicious, optimistic type like Linda insisted on going off alone with some strange geologists? But at last the weird black car purred quietly to a stop in front of the cabin, and Linda rushed in looking excited and happy. Just about as happy, it occurred to Dani, as she'd looked the day she heard about the wonderful cattle ranch they'd just inherited.

"Okay," Dani said in a sarcastic tone of voice. "What happened? Did they make a huge down payment?"

"No, not yet," Linda said. "They're seriously thinking about leasing the house for at least six months, but they have to find out a few things first. Like whether they can get a powerful enough generator and how long it would take to wire the house. They didn't seem to be too worried about anything else, but Mr. Smithson said they'd definitely have to have electricity because they'll need it for some of their equipment."

Dani threw up her hands. "Well, that's that," she said. "They'll never go to that much trouble to fix up a place they're just planning to live in for a few months."

But optimistic Linda was still hopeful. "I think they just might," she said, and then added wistfully, "Mrs. Smithson said she really loved the fireplace, and the verandas."

Dani shrugged and dropped the subject. At the same time she reminded herself not to even hope that they might get all that extra rent money. And that meant no chance of an allowance, which probably meant that there would never be enough money for two sets of bus tickets. So there was definitely going to have to be some other way.

As she waited to go to sleep that night she thought again about the stowaway possibility. She pictured just how it might work. She (or maybe even she and Stormy if he was still insisting on going) could pack some bags and hide them in one of the old junk cars in Gus's parking lot. And then she (or they) could hang around waiting for the right kind of truck to pull into the lot. Maybe a truckload of furniture, on its way to Reno with just a canvas covering stretched over its load. And then, while the driver was off somewhere, probably in the hotel bar flirting with Gloria, or maybe risking his health by visiting the world's filthiest public rest room at Greasy Gus's, they would grab their bags, scramble up under the canvas and hide themselves away in the load.

As she began to get sleepy, Dani could almost see herself curled up on a couch, or chair, snug and secure and safely hidden under the protecting canvas, bouncing along the long road to Reno. And after Reno? Well, maybe another truck, or perhaps, if they'd made it that far for free, there would be enough money to go the rest of the way by bus.

She was still thinking about the stowaway plan on Monday morning when, on her way to school, she decided to make a detour past Gus's parking lot, to size up the possibilities. Mostly just to pick out a handy junker car close to the parking area where they could hide out while they waited for the right truck to come along. But she had barely turned off the sidewalk when she saw something that made her gasp with excited surprise. Sitting there, only a few yards from the service station, was a truck that looked strangely like the one she'd been imagining only the night before. A slat-sided ranch truck with a huge canvas cover stretched over an uneven, angular load. A load that might very well include such things as tables and dressers—and maybe even a comfortable couch or chair.

Edging closer, she looked around cautiously. No one around in the parking lot, or among the dead cars, or even back in the dim, oily light inside Gus's garage. She moved closer and looked around again. Still no one in sight.

Another sideways sidle and she was behind the truck and checking out a place where the canvas cover seemed to be loose enough to permit someone to crawl under. But the truck bed was too high. Climbing in, or even peeking in, was not going to be easy. But once Dani made up her mind to do something, she wasn't easily discouraged, and at that moment she definitely had made up her mind to see what was under the canvas cover.

Backing cautiously away from the truck, she scouted around among Gus's junk heaps until she found a sturdy wooden crate. After she'd carried the heavy box back to the truck, she climbed up, stood on tiptoe and lifted one end of the cover. Lifted one side of the canvas, ducked her head under it, and suddenly found herself staring at a horrible sight.

Right in front of her face, a bald-headed, weather-beaten man with a wide thin-lipped mouth was lying on a folded mattress with his eyes tightly shut. The horrible possibility that the man was dead flashed through Dani's mind. And then an even more horrible possibility presented itself. He was alive and staring at her with bulging red-rimmed eyes. Before she could retreat the man's mouth opened in a snaggletoothed grin and a huge hand reached out to grab her shoulder. She struggled and tried to yell for help but her scream fizzled into a squeak and the grip on her shoulder only tightened. But then as she staggered backward and fell off the box, the hand lost its grip. Jumping to her feet, she ran. Ran frantically across the parking lot, across the street and into the nearest doorway, which happened to be the entrance to the Silver Grill Cafe.

She didn't stop to look back until she was safely inside the restaurant. With her heart still thumping crazily, she peered out from behind a Coca-Cola poster and watched as a huge bald-headed man crawled out of the back of the truck, looked around, stretched and yawned, climbed into the truck's cab and slammed the door. She stayed where she was, watching from inside the window until, a few minutes later, the truck pulled out of the parking lot and headed up the highway toward Reno.

It wasn't until sometime later, when she was again on her way to school, that she began to calm down enough to realize how silly her reaction had been. Pretty funny, really, to get that panicky just because a crabby old truck driver, who happened to look something like a Gila monster, didn't like her peeking into the back of his truck while he was taking a nap. She shrugged and actually laughed a little and, as she turned the corner, she almost managed to keep from looking back toward the parking lot, to be sure he was really gone. The truck was gone, all right, so that was the end of it. She wasn't going to let herself even think about it anymore. And she didn't, at least not much, and not while she was fully awake.

Dreams were harder to control. That very same night she woke up suddenly and sat straight up in bed, while parts of a crazy mixed-up dream tumbled through her mind. A dream about a truck driver who climbed out of the back of his truck and changed into a gigantic Gila monster right before her eyes. But it was only a dumb dream and she'd pretty much forgotten about it by the next day on the way home from school when Stormy brought up the subject in a roundabout way.

"Any rent money yet?" Stormy asked.

Dani laughed sarcastically. "No way," she said. "I told you to forget about those geologists renting our house. It's just not ever going to happen."

Stormy sighed. "I guess we'll have to stow away then. Huh?"

46

It wasn't until then that Dani knew for sure that stowing away on a truck was another thing that wasn't going to happen. At least not to her.

"No," she said firmly. "Stowing away is out too. And I don't want to talk about it."

chapter
7

So the possibility of stowing away was gone, and that left only one way out of Rattler Springs. And that was finding some way to add to the bus ticket fund. For the next day or so Dani spent a lot of time thinking about ways to do it. Both she and Stormy did. In fact, for the next day or two reading *White Fang* definitely took a backseat to moneymaking schemes. By Monday evening they'd come up with quite a few ideas, but no money at all unless you counted a silver dollar Stormy found in the slot machine in the bar.

On Wednesday the weather suddenly went from hot to an awful lot hotter. On the way home from school, Dani popped heat bubbles in the melting tar of Silver Avenue and watched mirages turn distant horizons into ghostly gray lakes. As she plodded along, the dry, shriveling heat ached in her lungs and pressed down like a heavy weight on her head and back. And when she kicked open the heat-warped front door of the cabin the air that surged out to meet her felt as if it came from the inside of an oven. Once inside she banged her books down on the coffee table, and an answering thump came from the back of the house.

For just a second she paused, listening and wondering. Linda, she knew, would still be at the bookstore. So who could it be? But of course she should have known. When she shoved open the kitchen door there he was, sitting at the table, clutching a big paper bag with one hand and a glass of water with the other. Dani frowned. "Hey," she said, "who let you in?"

Stormy's jack-o'-lantern face was flushed and sweaty. "Nobody," he said. "I just came on in. The door wasn't locked."

Dani threw up her hands. "Yeah, I know." The lock on the back door, like nearly everything else in the cabin, had stopped working a long time ago. "But that doesn't mean—"

"Hey. I got another idea," Stormy interrupted. "And lemons. I got lemons."

Dani stared, hands on hips. "What on earth are you blabbering about?"

"Lemons. For lemonade." Stormy rattled on, "You know. To sell, for bus money."

It took a while, but Dani finally began to get the picture. Stormy's silver dollar had been spent on lemons and what he had in mind was that he and Dani were going to set up a lemonade stand and make a whole lot of money for the bus tickets fund.

Dani never was wildly enthusiastic about the idea, not even right at first. For one thing it made her nervous that they were going to have to spend so much money buying stuff before they could even start to make any back.

"We'll have to buy paper cups," she told Stormy. "And one of those big bags of ice cubes from Gus's freezer."

"Naw, I'll get the ice," Stormy said. "From the bar."

Dani nodded, thinking rather reluctantly that maybe a lemonade stand wasn't such a bad idea after all. Especially if you had a business partner who had a free ice connection. So the ice and the lemons were taken care of, and the O'Donnells just happened to have a new bag of sugar. And Stormy knew where he could find two apple crates and a wide board to make the stand. But that still left deciding where to set it up. After a little thought Dani decided that the best place, in fact almost the only shady place in town, would be under the awning of the Grand Hotel.

So while Stormy set up the stand, Dani found an old cigar box for a cash drawer, and made a sign that said ICE COLD LEMONADE 10 CENTS A CUP. Linda came home while they were still in the kitchen, mixing up the first batch of lemonade. She looked hot and tired but after she'd splashed water on her face and arms she only watched without saying much until they were about to leave the house. Then she said she didn't mind investing some sugar in their enterprise, but she did hope her best pitcher didn't get broken.

It was after four o'clock by the time they got set up, and for a while business wasn't exactly brisk. Their first customers were Mrs. Graham and Ellie Blake, who stopped by on their way to the store. The third customer turned out to be none other than old Greasy Gus.

Gus, of Gus's garage and gas station, was big and bulgy and, according to rumor, just about the strongest man alive. And probably the ugliest too. The top of Gus's pear-shaped head was completely bald, but he had quite a lot of hair hanging down around the edges, as well as from his chin. He was tall and probably pretty fat, except that it was hard to tell for sure, because of all the overalls he wore. Even in hot weather Gus usually wore several layers of overalls. Greasy, ragged things with so many big holes in them it might have been embarrassing, except that the holes in one pair didn't match the holes in the others. At least not usually.

Most of the kids in Rattler Springs called Gus names and held their noses whenever they saw him, but Stormy always said Gus was his friend. Dani had wondered how bad your social life would have to be to choose someone like Greasy Gus for a friend, but she'd never said so to Stormy. It was the kind of thing she didn't like to waste energy fighting about.

It must have been around four-thirty when Gus came by on his way to the hotel bar. When he saw the lemonade stand he stopped and looked for a long time, grinning and muttering into his chin whiskers. Then he dug around in several overalls pockets until he found a dime and slapped it down on the counter. When he got his lemonade he slurped it down so fast that most of it dripped off the ends of his walrus mustache.

He disappeared into the bar then, but a little later, when he came back out, he stopped again and was even more enthusiastic.

"This here is what I like to see," he said. "Couple of whippersnappers setting up to do business instead of running around getting into trouble like some I might mention. Lookee here," he said to Lefty Morgan, the owner of Lefty's Bar, who just happened along about then. "Lookee here. Ain't this something."

Lefty, who seemed to be in a hurry, muttered under his breath and tried to get past, but Gus kept blocking his path and going on about the stuff he used to sell when he was a kid. It wasn't until Lefty broke down and bought some lemonade that Gus let him get away. After that he did more or less the same thing to Maude Harris when she came by on her way to the post office. It wasn't until he noticed a big, overheated Buick steaming into his service station that Gus bought another lemonade, added an extra ten cents as a tip and hurried back across the street. But a little while later he sent over a thirsty tourist family with four kids to drink lemonade while he worked on their broken-down car.

It was almost five o'clock when Dani counted what was in the cigar box and found out that they'd made enough to pay for the paper cups and the lemons already, and almost four dollars clear profit. But only a few minutes later disaster struck. A disaster named Ronnie Grabler.

Dani was just coming back from making up a new pitcher of lemonade when she noticed Stormy staring past her with a strange expression on his face. She whirled around and there, only a few yards away, was Ronnie Grabler. She turned away quickly, pretending she hadn't seen him and hoping Ronnie had something else—some other victim—in mind. But no such luck.

Ronnie was wearing khaki shorts and a filthy T-shirt with the sleeves rolled up into dirty white doughnuts, and his usual cowboy boots. Ronnie's big, expensive cowboy boots were kind of a joke at school because, as far as anyone knew, Ronnie had never been anywhere near a horse. It was the kind of joke, of course, that no one mentioned if Ronnie was around. But now the big dangerous boots were clumping up to the lemonade stand and their bowlegged wearer was saying, "Hey, hey. Look at the big businessmen. How's about a sample?"

"Ten cents," Stormy said in a grim tone of voice. Stormy's chin was set in a way that told Dani he was about to do something rash. Rash, and in this case very dangerous. Dani quickly poured a cup of lemonade and held it out to Ronnie. "Here," she said. "Take it. Take it and scram."

But Stormy's voice was louder and firmer. *"Ten cents,"* he kept on insisting.

Ronnie grabbed the cup out of Dani's hand, took a swallow or two and threw the rest out into the street. "Not too bad," he said, "but, hey, I'm a little short on cash right now." Then his sweaty face lit up in an especially evil grin. "But I won't be soon as I collect some rent money that I got coming. Some rent money that I got coming 'cause some little squatters set up their lemonade business on Grabler property. Right here on my dad's sidewalk space."

It probably wasn't true. Dani was pretty sure that public

sidewalks don't belong to the buildings they happen to be in front of. But when she said so Ronnie only shrugged and said, "They do if I say they do. And besides, even if the sidewalk isn't our property, that there awning sure enough is. So the shade is ours too. And you little bums been swipin' our private shade all afternoon." His eyes moved to the cigar box. "Way I figure it, shade gets pretty pricey on a day like this so—"

"How much?" Dani interrupted grimly. It wasn't fair but there was no use trying to argue with a muscle-bound lump-head like Ronnie Grabler. Particularly when the lump-head's father owned half the block. She was moving toward the cigar box when suddenly Stormy pushed her away, grabbed the money box and ran. And a second later Ronnie took off after him bellowing, "Come back here, dummy," and some other insulting stuff. Stormy was yelling too, a high-pitched yelping sound like a scared puppy.

For a few seconds, while Stormy and then Ronnie crossed the highway and disappeared from view behind the gas station, Dani stayed right where she was. But then the noises, which were floating back across the highway, took on a shriller and more desperate sound. Changed into the high-pitched shrieking of someone who was scared to death, or maybe getting pounded to a pulp. A picture appeared before Dani's eyes, a picture of Stormy sinking down to the ground under a rain of ferocious blows, and suddenly she was running too. She didn't have the slightest idea what she was going to do when she caught up with them, but somebody had to do something —in a hurry.

She could tell now that the yelling was coming from Gus's garage, but as she rounded the station, dodging old tires and car parts, the howls had a different pitch and tone. By the time she dashed into the garage she was beginning to wonder if the howler was still Stormy. And sure enough, it wasn't.

The first thing Dani saw when her eyes had adjusted to the dim light of the garage was Gus standing beside his famous grease pit holding something big and heavy down over the edge. Dani had heard all the stories about how strong Gus was, but if she hadn't seen it herself she wouldn't have believed that anybody could dangle a big kid over the edge of a grease pit by the back of his khaki shorts. But that was what Gus was doing. Standing there straddle legged, holding the struggling, howling Ronnie with just one hand, he was grinning his snaggletoothed grin while, on the other side of the pit, Stormy grinned back, still clutching the cigar box to his chest.

When Gus finally pulled Ronnie out of the pit and put him back on his feet he slunk off across the highway, stopping only once to glare back threateningly at Dani and Stormy. Dani knew the threat was a real one, so the second Ronnie disappeared into the hotel she grabbed Stormy and headed for home. Stopping only long enough to rescue Linda's pitcher from under the hotel awning, they made it back to Dani's house without any more Grabler trouble. Linda was cooking dinner in the stifling heat of the kitchen so they sat on the back steps, drank up what was left of the lemonade, counted their money and talked about what had happened. Talked and snickered every time they thought about Ronnie and the grease pit. After a while Dani stopped laughing.

"Okay," she said. "It was pretty funny but it won't last, you know. Old Ronnie might be scared off for the time being, but he'd be right back if we tried it again."

Stormy gulped, swallowed another snicker and stared at her. "I know," he said. "He'll wait until Gus is busy, and then—"

"Well, anyway," Dani said, "we were pretty lucky to get out of the lemonade business while we were still ahead. I mean, four dollars is better than nothing, even if it's not going to make much of a difference in . . ." She looked back through the screen door to where Linda was doing something with hamburger that smelled pretty good. Lowering her voice to a whisper, she went on, ". . . in the running-away fund."

Stormy sighed. "I know. But it *was* a good idea. Gus thought the lemonade stand was a real good moneymaking idea."

"Yeah." Dani chuckled sarcastically. "He sure did. Greasy Gus, the world-famous moneymaking expert."

Stormy frowned uncertainly. "Gus is my—"

"I know," Dani interrupted. "Gus is your friend."

Stormy's frown deepened and for a while no one said anything more. Stormy was still probably trying to decide whether to slug Dani for calling Gus greasy. And Dani? Dani was thinking that whatever you thought about Gus, he had been a pretty good friend to Stormy when Stormy really needed one.

Thinking about needing friends led to wondering about why Stormy had gotten himself into such a mess. How he'd had the nerve to snatch the money box from right under the nose of someone as big and mean as Ronnie Grabler.

Of course it might have been that Stormy was just too dumb to know what a risk he was taking. Or else it might simply have been stubbornness. Everybody knew that Stormy Arigotti was major-league stubborn, so that probably was a big part of it. But then again, maybe it had something to do with —guts? With the fact that, along with being stubborn and reckless, Stormy Arigotti was also a pretty gutsy kid.

For some reason it was kind of an intriguing idea. So intriguing, in fact, that for a moment Dani actually thought about telling Stormy what she'd been thinking. But the more she thought about it, the harder it got to come up with the right words. In the end she didn't tell him anything, but she did surprise herself by going in to ask Linda if Stormy could stay for dinner.

Linda said, "Certainly," which wasn't much of a surprise since she was always worrying about Stormy's Beer Nuts and pretzel diet. And Stormy said, "Wow, would I!" which was no surprise at all.

chapter
8

The night after the lemonade disaster Dani was awakened twice by horribly realistic nightmares. The first one was a lot like a dream she'd had before. A dream in which she was minding her own business when suddenly a hand grabbed her shoulder and whirled her around to face a man wearing an oily denim jacket and a Gila monster's head. The second dream started out just about the same but this time the strange creature had the body of a Gila monster—fat, scaly body, clawed hands and feet—and the head of Ronnie Grabler. It was a pretty awful combination.

What with the lemonade fiasco and the nightmares, Dani had completely forgotten about the possibility of getting an allowance when some very peculiar things started happening. The first strange event was when she looked out her front window just in time to see the geologists' weird car heading into town on Silver Avenue. And the next day, there it was again, this time going out toward the ranch. And then on Monday, Linda came home from the bookstore with amazing news. The Smithsons had definitely decided to lease the ranch for six months if they could wire the house and hook it up to a generator. And they really were willing to pay seventy-five dollars a month.

Dani couldn't believe it. She had been so sure that the whole thing had been just another one of Linda's "happily ever after" pipe dreams. But now it looked as if it was really going to happen. By the middle of the next week Linda had signed a lease contract and picked up her first seventy-five-dollar check. It was great to get all that extra money but, as it turned out, Dani didn't get any of it. There were, it seemed, too many overdue bills to be taken care of first. But her mother did say, "I really do think someone your age should have an allowance, if it's at all possible. So we'll see what we can do next month."

Not till next month. Dani had stomped away angrily and later she told Stormy, "Next month will be too late. I've— We've got to get started a long time before that. Even if she'd let me have a huge allowance, like a couple of dollars a week, I won't—I mean we won't—have enough money for the bus tickets until way past the middle of summer." At least not enough for two tickets, she added silently. Out loud she only said, "I wanted to get started right away, like before school gets out. I said I was going to leave right away, and I meant it."

She had meant it, and she still did. That day in the grave-yard when she'd yelled at the sky, she'd definitely meant to start off immediately. Like in a day or two. And at that moment she hadn't felt frightened at all—only fiercely determined. But somehow putting it off had made the whole thing seem less like a real possibility, and also a lot more dangerous. As if, now that the desert had been warned, it would have time to think up ways to stop her. And the longer she had to wait the more time she spent thinking of things that might go wrong.

On the other hand, she had to admit that it might be slightly interesting to hang around Rattler Springs just a little longer. Long enough, at least, to see what the geologists were actually going to do way out there in Linda's run-down, dusty old ranch house.

The first thing they did was to truck in a lot of heavy equipment. Only a few days after the Smithsons paid their first month's rent, a lot of trucks began to head up Silver Avenue in the direction of the ranch. Big trucks that seemed to be carrying all kinds of lumber and strange-looking machinery. Linda said she thought the machinery was just the generator and maybe some scientific equipment, but other people had other ideas about what it might be.

One of the trucks looked like a big, long moving van. Dani was heading up Silver Avenue and just passing the Grand Hotel when the van went by. It was so long that it had to back and turn to get around the corner and for a while it got kind of hung up. Dani stopped to watch and before long some other people did too.

One of the first ones to show up was Stormy, of course, and a little later most of the people who'd been in the bar straggled out. Even Stormy's mother, Gorgeous Gloria, came out and joined the crowd, wearing a stretchy red dress with a silver thread woven into it, and still carrying a dish towel and the glass she'd been drying. After a while Dani got bored with the truck and started watching Gloria instead. It was interesting because you didn't see Stormy's mother out-of-doors very often, at least during the daytime.

Dani had always thought that Gloria Arigotti was very young looking to be the mother of a great big nine-year-old kid like Stormy. She had a movie-star-type figure and lots of superblond hair, and she always wore very glamorous-looking clothing, like tight sweaters and short skirts. But seeing her now in the bright sunshine Dani could see how she might be pretty old after all. Like maybe even thirty, which was nearly as old as Dani's mother.

Gloria was chatting and joking with some of the other people who'd come out of the bar to watch. People, men mostly, seemed to enjoy talking to Gloria even though the rumor was that she could be pretty dangerous at times. Like getting mad at somebody and trying to hit them with a whiskey bottle. Or like the time she'd showed up at the O'Donnells' in the middle of the night, yelling and screaming because she thought Stormy was staying over without permission. He hadn't been there, so she'd gone off without him, but the next day he showed up with a black eye. Linda, who always worried about Stormy having a lousy mother, had been sure that Gloria had done it. Dani believed Stormy when he said he'd bumped into a door, and she'd told Linda so. She'd reminded Linda that the little klutz was always bumping into something or other, and she'd also hinted about how there were a lot of different ways to be a lousy parent. Right now, for instance, watching Gloria, it seemed to Dani that it might be kind of exciting to have such a glamorous mother.

Dani was still watching Gloria and the rest of the crowd and thinking about a town where there wasn't anything more exciting to do than watch a stalled moving van, when someone punched her in the back. Hard. Not angry hard, actually, but just Stormy's usual tooth-rattling substitute for a normal person's "Hi" or "Hey, you."

"Hey, watch it," Dani said crossly, but then she saw his face and added, "What's up?" Judging by his expression, something important definitely was.

There was a suspicious squint to Stormy's eyes and his voice hissed excitedly when he said, "They're spies. That's what they are. Spies."

Dani was puzzled. "What are you talking about? Who are spies?"

"Those ge—geo—" Giving up on *ge-ol-o-gists*, Stormy went on, "Those guys who are renting your ranch."

"Oh yeah?" She couldn't help grinning. "What makes you think they're spies?"

"Because . . ." Stormy rolled his eyes around thoughtfully, and went on rolling them until Dani threatened to thump him on the head to get him started. "You know," he finally said, "like in that book. The one about Jerry and the Nazi?"

"Jerry?" For a moment Dani couldn't imagine what he was talking about, but then she began to get the picture. A year or so ago Stormy had been hung up on a series of dumb stories about this kid named Jerry who was supposed to be some kind of a superdetective. Even though he was only twelve years old he went around solving complicated mysteries about all sorts of criminals like cat burglars and smugglers. And there had been one story in which Jerry discovered that an apparently innocent toy maker was really a Nazi spy who hid government secrets inside his dolls and teddy bears. All the books were pretty unbelievable and the spy story had been especially stupid. She'd been glad when Stormy finally got tired of them, but now here he was back to imagining that he was Jerry, the detective.

"Oh, I get it," she said, grinning. "Look, Stormy. The war's over. The Nazis got wiped out. Or hadn't you heard?"

Stormy glared. "I know that. But there's other kinds of spies besides Nazi ones. Gus thinks so too. Gus says, why do they have to have all that scientific equipment just to look for minerals and stuff in the ground. Gus says he knows a guy who did that all his life, and all he needed was a donkey and a pickax."

Dani shrugged angrily. Actually she was getting a little bit tired of all the famous quotations from Gus. Ever since the day when old Ronnie got dangled over the grease pit it seemed like all Stormy could talk about was his friend Gus. And as if hearing about Gus the champion muscle man wasn't boring enough, now there was Gus the geologist. For some reason Dani found the whole thing pretty infuriating. Not that she wouldn't be glad if Stormy found someone else to tag around after. Definitely not. As far as she was concerned that would be just great. And if Gus wanted to finish reading *White Fang* out loud, that would be great too. That is, if he *could* read, which probably wasn't a safe bet.

"Look," she said. "There's nothing mysterious about the Smithsons. They just happen to be perfectly innocent geologists. Everybody with any sense knows that."

But the next day it turned out that everybody didn't. At least not at Rattler Springs school. The favorite topic of conversation at school that day, and pretty much all that week, was what the Smithsons were up to, out there at the ranch. Bob Bailey said he'd heard they were government agents looking for a place to test atom bombs. And some other kids seemed to think the Smithsons were counterfeiters, and the stuff in one of those big trucks had been presses for printing money. But the craziest idea was Clara Mason's.

Clara, who was the only other girl in the seventh grade besides Dani, was a horror-story nut who was always reading about vampires and demons and monsters. And it was her idea that the Smithsons were really Frankenstein types, and all that machinery was some kind of monster assembly line.

Dani thought the whole thing was pretty ridiculous. "Look," she told Bob, and a couple of other people who happened to be standing around listening. "Just because their clothes don't look like they bought them at a rummage sale, and they drive a custom-made car, doesn't make them into some kind of mad scientists. It just makes them a little bit different than most of the people around here. Okay? And you know who's always suspicious of anyone who's a little bit different? Hicks and hillbillies, that's who."

It was the truth but, as usual, no one appreciated it much. In fact, when she told them that stuff about hicks and hillbillies Bob muttered, "Okay. So I'm a hick. I'd rather be a hick than a stuck-up know-it-all." And of course some of the other kids who heard what he said went around the rest of the day making cracks about stuck-up know-it-alls.

It wasn't fair. Just because Dani wasn't a natural-born desert rat, and because she got pretty good grades without having to study much, the other kids at Rattler Springs Elementary School thought she was conceited.

She walked home that day telling herself she wasn't ever going to try to tell anybody at that crummy school anything ever again. It wasn't the first time she'd told herself to keep her mouth shut about how she felt about living in Rattler Springs. But then somebody would start teasing her and she'd forget and start shooting her mouth off again.

Sometimes, when she cooled off, she knew that a lot of her problems at the Rattler Springs school were her own fault. She knew that the reason she got teased so much was because she'd gotten off on the wrong foot when she first came, complaining about everything and bragging about how much better it had been back home. Of course, she'd only been a stupid little homesick eight-year-old at the time, but she still ought to have known better. And she certainly ought to know better now than to go around calling people hillbillies and hicks. But she'd done it, and she knew that for the next few days she was going to have to pay for it.

The next morning she thought about staying home with a planned stomachache. Not an imaginary stomachache. She didn't go in for imaginary stuff. A planned one. And she probably would have except that at eight o'clock it was already over a hundred degrees in her bedroom and it was obviously going to be a lot hotter before the day was over. So she gritted her teeth and went to school—and nobody even mentioned stuck-up know-it-alls. Or anything else about Dani O'Donnell.

Not that the Rattler Springs student body had suddenly turned over a new leaf. Not a chance. What made the difference was that they suddenly had somebody else to torment. Somebody named Portia Alexandria Smithson.

——— chapter ———
9

Portia Alexandria Smithson was as skinny and blond as her geologist parents and, like theirs, her features were normal enough, but nothing special. All except for her eyes and ears. Her eyes were big and round and bright blue and her ears were big too, and stuck out on each side through wispy blond hair. She looked okay but definitely different and, as Dani had good reason to know, different was dangerous in Rattler Springs.

For one thing her clothes were all wrong. She came into the sweltering, sweaty classroom that first morning wearing a fancy, long-sleeved white blouse, with a monogram on the pocket and trimmed around the collar and cuffs with blue braid. Her skirt, also blue, was sharply pleated, and her saddle shoes looked brand new. It was an outfit that might have been terrific at some big-city school, but the reaction in Rattler

Springs was . . . Looking around the classroom, Dani felt like she was watching a bunch of alley cats reacting to the new cat on the block. It was easy to conjure up a mental image of arching backs and bristling tails. You could, that is, if you were interested in that kind of imagining stuff, which Dani definitely wasn't.

The expression on the new girl's face when Mr. Graham had her stand up to be introduced was different too. "Boys and girls," Mr. Graham said, "I'd like you to meet our new fifth-grade student, Portia Smithson." He went on then being humorous about how lucky they were that Portia was a girl because the upper grades were short on girls, and long, "or at least heavy," on boys. Then he looked at Ronnie and Bob, who were pretty "heavy," all right, and everybody snickered. Everyone except Dani and the new girl, at least. Dani didn't snicker because it wasn't particularly funny, and the new girl didn't either. But, on the other hand, she didn't look as nervous as you might expect.

What you'd expect, under the circumstances, was a certain amount of terror, and for a second she did look a little bit scared. But almost immediately Dani began to get the feeling that even that little bit wasn't for real. It was as if the whole thing, the clasped hands and down-turned eyes, was an act. It was pretty believable, except now and then when the eyes flashed up and around the room and then quickly dropped back down.

It must have been those fiery glances that made Dani curious enough to decide to talk to the new girl as soon as possible. At least curiosity was part of it. The other part just might have been a little bit of sympathy for someone else who was coming to the Rattler Springs school and getting off on the wrong foot. Coming possibly from some big-city school, maybe even a private one, judging by the school uniform look of her clothing. It had been bad enough for Dani, and she'd be willing to bet it was going to be even worse for this poor kid. So at the first recess Dani followed Portia Smithson out onto the playground.

Just outside the door she grabbed the new girl's arm and said, "Hi, Portia. My name is Dani. Dani O'Donnell."

The big eyes were wide, and at that moment, as blank as a painted doll's. "Hi, Dani," the girl breathed in a feathery whisper. "But my name is Pixie now. I haven't been Portia for a long time."

Dani looked Portia/Pixie/whoever over with increased interest. "Okay then, Pixie," she said. Grabbing the other girl by the sleeve, she pulled her back toward the schoolhouse wall, away from some fifth- and sixth-graders who were hanging around staring. There were five or six of them, all boys except for Jeannie Wallace. "Scram," Dani yelled, and then waited for their reluctant retreat before she said, "Just look at them, standing around goggle-eyed just because you're new." She sighed. "That's the way it always is here. Don't you hate it? Don't you hate being here?"

The eyes flashed a signal that, again, Dani didn't quite get. Anger maybe, or perhaps just curiosity. But the voice was more like little-girl wonder. "Do *you* hate it?" she asked.

"Sure I do. The school, the whole town, everything." Dani looked the new girl over again, checking out the pleated skirt, the stiff new shoes and the wide-eyed, innocent stare. "You know. The whole place. All of it." She gestured, taking in the schoolyard and on and on, clear out to the distant hills. "Gruesome, isn't it?"

Portia's eyes followed the gesture. "Yes. Yes, it is gruesome," she said eagerly. "It's probably the most gruesome place I've ever been."

A puzzling thought occurred to Dani. "Hey, why'd you come? To the school I mean. It's going to be summer vacation in a couple of weeks. Couldn't you have skipped the rest of the year? I'll bet you're way ahead of the fifth grade here."

"Well, yes. I guess I could have . . . ," the new girl started to say, when the noise level on the playground suddenly went up to a deafening roar. It sounded like a riot but it was probably just that the little kids had been let out for recess. Dani started to check to see if that was it, but before she'd even gotten completely turned around something hit her in the middle of the back. "This is Stormy," she said without even looking.

They were almost the same height, Stormy and the new girl, although Stormy was a lot heavier. Standing only a few feet away, he was staring as if he'd seen a ghost. "Hey." Dani thumped him on the head to get his attention. "This is Por—Pixie. Pixie Smithson, she's in the fifth grade."

"Yeah, Smithson. I heard." Stormy nodded and gulped before he started to say, "The ge—ge—"

"Geologists," Dani said. She turned to Pixie. "That's right, isn't it? Your folks are the geologists, aren't they? The ones who are renting my mom's ranch house?"

"Your mom's ranch house? We're renting your house?" Pixie's face registered surprise. At least it looked like surprise. Dani was definitely getting the feeling that Pixie's face was not going to be all that easy to read. Stormy's, on the other hand, was only too easy, and what it was registering at the moment was suspicion and something pretty close to shock.

"Are you—I mean—are your folks really spies?"

"Yeah, spies? Are they spies?" another voice chimed in, and it wasn't until then that Dani noticed that the fifth- and sixth-grade bunch had edged its way back into hearing distance. It was Eddie Bailey, Bob's sixth-grade brother, who was asking. "Are you guys really spies?"

Pixie looked bewildered. "Spies?" Turning to Dani, she said, "What do they mean, spies?"

But just at that moment the bell rang for the end of the upper grades' recess. On their way back to the classroom Dani whispered, "It's just a stupid rumor. I guess some of the kids are saying that your folks are spies." She laughed. "And that's just for starters. There's a whole lot of even more ridiculous stuff going around."

Pixie hung back, asking questions like "What kind of stuff?" "Who said it?" and "What did they say?"

So Dani began to explain but she hardly got into the rumors about the counterfeit money printing press, and barely mentioned the one about Frankenstein-type scientists. Pixie was obviously interested, hanging on to Dani's arm to keep her from leaving, and asking all kinds of questions.

"Hey, we've got to go in," Dani told her finally. "Mr. Graham is really fussy about coming in after the second bell.

I'll tell you some more later." One thing she especially wanted to tell Pixie was that she'd just have to get used to the fact that in crummy little hick towns like Rattler Springs people didn't have anything better to do than make up stupid rumors about everything and everybody.

Back at her seat Dani got out her math book, checked the seventh-grade assignment on the board and started to work. But every now and then she glanced back at the fifth-grade corner, where, considering the fact that she'd just been accused of being a spy or something even worse, Pixie was behaving in a surprisingly normal manner. Watching her, Dani felt puzzled and strangely fascinated.

It was partly, she told herself, a certain amount of sympathy for someone who was going to be going through a lot of the same kind of Rattler Springs torment that she'd been through her own self. But there was more to it than that. Some of it was how hard the new girl was to figure out. Usually when you met new people you started forming a kind of mental picture of them right off the bat. Sometimes the picture changed later on, but it tended to be a gradual kind of thing. The Pixie picture seemed to be nothing but changes. A change every split second. Like one of those little moving-picture books that you flip with your thumbnail, and as the pages turn a figure runs and jumps, or a face smiles and frowns. That was it, she decided. That was what the new girl made her think of. A thumbnail movie book.

When Mr. Graham dismissed the class that afternoon he called the new girl up to his desk to "go over a list of books and supplies you're going to need." At least that was what he said he wanted to talk to her about, but Dani thought there was more to it than that. Watching Mr. Graham and the Portia/Pixie character chatting away while most of the class dawdled and fooled around on their way out, Dani wondered if what he really was doing was trying to keep the new girl from being picked on. Trying to keep her safely in the room until some of the most dangerous types, like Ronnie Grabler, for instance, had given up and gone on home.

After a while Dani pretended to give up too and went outside. She was still walking very slowly toward the road when Pixie finally came out.

"Wait. Wait a minute, Dani." Pixie was running after her. "I have to talk to you."

What Pixie wanted to talk about, of course, was all the rumors about her folks. "Tell me about it again," she said eagerly. "All that stuff about spies and monster machines."

But Dani had just gotten started when Pixie said, "Uh-oh. Got to go," and ran toward the road. Crawling toward them through a floating sea of dust and heat waves was the strange vehicle that was somewhere between a tank and a Cadillac. When it coasted quietly to a stop, a door opened and Pixie disappeared inside.

chapter

10

Walking home that afternoon, Dani moved as slowly as a desert tortoise. The heat pressed down like a heavy hand on her head and shoulders, but that wasn't the only problem. On that particular day there was also something weighing on her mind too. Something known as Portia—or Pixie—Smithson. But the heat must have messed up her brain, because she hadn't come up with a single useful conclusion by the time she reached Silver Avenue.

Was poor little Pixie really as calm and unconcerned as she'd seemed? And if she was—was it because she was really that brave? Or was it just that she was too stupid to know how much trouble she was in? When Dani was nearly home she suddenly decided to make a little detour past the bookstore so she could ask Linda a question or two that might help to clear things up.

The dusty little bookstore was, as usual this time of year, incredibly hot and almost empty. Seated behind Mr. Cooley's beat-up old desk, Linda was reading a book, while her heat-frizzled hair framed her face in a halo of curly corkscrews. Nobody else was in sight.

"Hey, Mom," Dani said, forgetting for the moment that she had decided, nearly a year before, that she wouldn't call her mother Mom again until she started acting more like a responsible parent. Started doing something responsible, for instance, to get herself and her only kid out of the desert and back where they belonged. "Hey, Mom," she said. "Did you know that those geologists had a kid? You never said anything to me about it."

Linda looked up from her book. "Why, yes, I think Mrs. Smithson mentioned a daughter. Ten years old, I think she said. But I believe she's staying with her grandmother and she won't be joining them for quite a while. Not till the fall term, I think Emily said."

Dani shrugged. "Oh yeah? Well, I guess somebody changed their minds. Because she's here right now."

"Who's here?"

"The daughter. She's in the fifth grade and her name is Portia. When it isn't Pixie, that is."

Linda looked puzzled, and she was still looking puzzled when Dani left the store and headed for home. She was in the alley between the general store and the post office when out of nowhere Stormy was walking beside her. Out of nowhere like always, but at least this time he didn't whack her on the back.

"Hi," he said. "What did she tell you?"

Dani pretended she didn't know what he was talking about. "What did who tell me?" she asked.

"That new girl. I saw you talking to her after school. What did she say about being a spy?"

"Oh, that," Dani said. "She didn't exactly say. But I don't think they're spies. What I think is that they're more like crazy scientists who make monsters out of dead people. You know, like Dr. Frankenstein. You remember when I told you about Frankenstein?" Right after she said it, Dani wondered why she'd told Stormy the Smithsons might be Frankenstein-type scientists. Of course she herself had gotten the idea from old ghost-crazy Clara, but she had to admit there was no special reason she had to repeat it to Stormy.

If Linda had been there she'd probably have said the reason was just Dani's "natural-born contrariness." Contrariness, according to Linda, was when a person took one point of view just because the other person was taking the opposite one. There had been times, not often but just now and then, when Dani might have confessed to a certain amount of contrariness, but this wasn't one of them. She hadn't said Frankenstein just because Stormy was saying spies. It was just that she was getting bored with spy stories, and a couple of crazy monster producers seemed, for the time being, a little more original. But what she hadn't counted on was Stormy's reaction.

"Yeah?" he said. "Yeah?" Then he just stood there wide-eyed and openmouthed for several seconds before he said,

"They're Frankensteins? Frankensteins. Wow!" Then except for an occasional "Wow!" he didn't say anything more until they got to Dani's house. In the stifling heat of the kitchen he got himself a glass of water and somehow managed to go on looking stunned and horror-struck while he drank it. It wasn't until he'd finished and put down the glass that he said, "Dani. Tell me about Frankenstein again. Okay?"

There was something about the look in Stormy's eyes that made Dani a little nervous. A kind of stiff, fish-eyed look, like somebody who'd just seen a ghost. "What about *White Fang*?" she asked. "We'd better finish *White Fang* before it's overdue."

But Stormy went on insisting until she broke down and told him, as briefly as she could, about how a scientist called Dr. Frankenstein made a monster out of pieces of dead people and how he built an electric machine that sort of shocked the monster into life and then the monster went around getting into trouble. Because the look in Stormy's eyes was already so strange she purposely tried to do a fairly tame and boring version of the story. She didn't, for instance, go into the way Boris Karloff had looked in the movie, which had been shown at the town hall a year or so ago, and which Dani remembered pretty well. But even the boring version really seemed to grab Stormy's attention. He went on staring with glassy eyes and asking dumb questions like "What did the monster eat?" and then, even more fish-eyed, "Did he eat people?"

At last Dani just stopped answering. Making a quick trip to her impossibly hot bedroom, she retrieved *White Fang* and got out again without breathing, so as not to broil her tonsils. Outside, on the back steps, where it was still hot but a little less unbearable, she started reading out loud. It took a while but, just as she'd planned, Stormy couldn't resist for long. After only a minute or two the back door creaked open. Stormy sat down beside her and went into his usual listening trance.

Dani went on reading until Linda came home, even though half of her mind went on fooling around with the Pixie thing, instead of really paying close attention to what the story was saying. It sounded all right to her but it must have made a difference to Stormy because as he was going home that night he said thanks as usual and then added, "Thanks for sort of reading to me."

And when Dani wanted to know what he meant by that crack, he shrugged and said, "I don't know. But it sounds realer sometimes. I like when it sounds real."

Some nerve, Dani thought. Here she'd been sitting out there on the splintery steps with the sweat running down her face for almost an hour and that was all the thanks she got. She thought about yelling after him, "Okay, you can read the rest of it yourself." She was still thinking about yelling when Stormy disappeared into the back door of the hotel.

It took Dani a long time to get to sleep that night, what with the heat and all the things she had to think about. Some of the things she thought about were the mean tricks the Rattler Springs kids had played on her when she was new and how they'd probably do the same things to Pixie. Tricks like slashing her bicycle tires and throwing apple cores or rotten tomatoes at her on her way home from school, or like hanging a dead rattlesnake over her front gate so she almost reached out and touched it before she realized what it was. The snake thing had happened because someone had gone to the trouble to find out that Dani had a kind of phobia about snakes. And if they'd gone to that much trouble for a mere "stuck-up know-it-all," who knew what they'd come up with for a foreign spy? Or a kid from a family of Frankensteins, for that matter. If she were Pixie Smithson, Dani decided, she would have a planned stomachache that would last until school was out for the summer.

But the next day Pixie was there in class, and the day after that too, and to Dani's surprise nothing much happened. Dani did notice some of the usual classroom teasing, whispered remarks and insulting faces. One time when Ronnie walked past Pixie's desk on his way to the pencil sharpener he made a monster face by pushing up on his nose and pulling down on the corners of his eyes. Some of the other kids gasped or giggled, but Pixie only looked vaguely pleased, as if she thought Grabler's disgusting face was some kind of classroom entertainment. But except for the whispers and ugly faces, not much new-kid-type teasing was happening. Dani couldn't understand it.

Of course, one big difference was that Pixie didn't have to walk to school. Instead of having to walk right through town past several houses, Lefty's Bar, the bank and the Grand Hotel, any one of which could provide shelter for a tomato thrower or a rattlesnake smuggler, Pixie Smithson was delivered almost to the front door of the schoolhouse every morning and picked up in the same spot every afternoon. That explained a lot, Dani decided. If she, Dani O'Donnell, had arrived at school every day in an automobile that looked like a Sherman tank, she probably could have managed to stay pretty calm too.

The other possible reason was pretty funny, actually. That possibility was that the usual new-kid tormentors had made up so many scary rumors that they'd scared themselves off. I mean if you really thought the kid who sat next to you in school was Dr. Frankenstein's daughter, you just might not want to get her especially mad at you.

But Dani was still curious. Curious enough to arrange chance meetings at recess time, or in the classroom before the last bell rang. Dani usually began the conversation with questions about the ranch house. Like how Pixie liked living there, and whether the new generator was working all right. The conversations were always brief and not very private so there was no chance to lead into the questions she really wanted to ask. But one afternoon—a Thursday—all that changed.

chapter

11

Dani was on her way home from school on Thursday when, just as she started up Silver Avenue, the Smithsons' car, or the Tank, as some people had started calling it, went past, slowed, backed up and pulled to a stop only a few feet away. As Dani stared in surprise, a back door flew open and Pixie ran toward her.

"Hi," she said and, grabbing Dani's arm, she led her around to the driver's window. The driver, the same thin-faced man Dani remembered seeing through the holey drapes, nodded and smiled. The smile was a little stiff maybe, but not particularly creepy. Certainly not what you'd expect from a foreign spy. Or a Frankenstein-type scientist, for that matter.

"Father," Pixie was saying, "this is Dani O'Donnell. You know, Mrs. O'Donnell's daughter."

The man nodded again and said, "Hello, Dani. Portia has been telling me all about you."

For the next second or two while Pixie was jabbering away Dani was so busy taking in all the fancy dials and thingamajigs on the car's dashboard that she didn't quite get what Pixie was talking about. But when she did begin to listen she heard, ". . . so I thought maybe I could visit with you until then. Would that be okay?"

"Visit me? Right now?" Dani said. "Oh, sure. That's okay." Without waiting to hear anything more, Pixie's father nodded, waved, put the Tank into gear and took off.

It wasn't until then that Dani learned what she'd just agreed to. What Pixie had been asking was if it would be all right for her to stay with Dani from the time school let out until five o'clock—every day. Her father, it seemed, had to be in town every weekday afternoon around five, and if he could wait until then to pick Pixie up it would save him from having to make an extra trip. And since her parents already knew Dani's mother they had agreed that the O'Donnells' house would be the best place for Pixie to wait.

Well, Dani thought when she finally understood, best for Pixie maybe, but right off the bat she had some doubts about just how good the arrangement was going to be for her.

On the good side, seeing so much of Pixie might be a great way to find out a lot of stuff she, and a bunch of other people, had been curious about. And it also might be just a little bit like it used to be back in Sea Grove when she had friends who visited after school, something that never had happened here in Rattler Springs. Oh, there was Stormy, of course, but he didn't count because he was a boy, and too young, and too—Stormy.

On the bad side, however, she could see right away that there might be some serious complications. She started trying to warn Pixie about one of them as they went on up Silver Avenue. "You know," she said, "there might be a problem about us walking home together every day."

Pixie looked puzzled. "It's not all that far. And you have to do it anyway, don't you?"

"I know," Dani said. "But it may not be easy." She went on to tell about the kinds of things that happened to unpopular kids in Rattler Springs. She was telling about the slashed bicycle tires when Pixie interrupted.

"Oh, do you ride a bicycle to school sometimes?" she asked.

Dani snorted. "Not lately. I ran out of money for new inner tubes." She could have gone on to say that there were a lot of other things wrong with her old bike, like rust and broken spokes, and brakes that usually didn't work. But that seemed to be beside the point so she started telling about the rotten tomatoes and dead rattlesnake instead. "That only happened when I first got here though," she admitted. "After a while they got bored with it, I guess." She grinned. "Or else they ran out of tomatoes and rattlesnakes."

"Tomatoes and rattlesnakes?" Pixie repeated, sounding amazed and, strangely enough, almost enthusiastic. "You think they might start doing things like that again because of me?" Dani said she wouldn't be surprised, and then Pixie actually said, "Oh, I hope so. I've never seen a rattlesnake before." Dani stared. She couldn't believe it. At least she wouldn't have been able to if she hadn't already started getting used to Pixie's strange reactions.

Another of Pixie's reactions that wasn't what you might expect concerned the historic old Jerky Joe cabin, the poor ragged wreck of a place where Dani and her mother lived. One of the reasons that Dani hadn't been too thrilled with the daily visit idea was because she didn't much like letting Pixie see the inside of the cabin. Actually she didn't much like to let anyone see it, but she could just imagine what a person like Pixie would think. A person whose parents could afford to pay seventy-five dollars a month for an old wreck of a house and, on top of that, buy a generator and pay to have the whole house wired for electricity. What would someone with that kind of money think of a kitchen counter covered with peeling linoleum and a bathroom that had a rusty tin shower instead of a tub? Not to mention those horrible holey drapes in the combination living room—bedroom. Dani couldn't help wincing when she thought about those drapes. But then Pixie walked into the cottage and acted like the place was some sort of palace. Well, maybe not a palace so much as a "fascinating place to live."

"What a fascinating place to live," Pixie said when they arrived in the tiny living room. "I love it. I'd love to live in a place like this."

"Fascinating?" Dani was amazed, and immediately suspicious. But Pixie didn't look like she was trying to be funny, or sarcastic either. Dani shrugged, rolling her eyes and throwing out her hands. "I think it's gruesome. Just look at it." She gestured at the daybed couch and the falling-apart drapes. "Disgusting."

"Oh no," Pixie said. "I've always wanted to live in a house like this. It's like—like something in one of my favorite books. I used to play a game about it."

"A book? What kind of book?" Dani asked.

"Well, there's this one story about these five kids whose father is dead and they live with their mother in this old—this old . . ." She stuttered to a stop then as if she had just decided not to go on with what she'd started.

She was still stammering when a loud voice said, "What's she doing here?" And there was Stormy, staring at them from the kitchen door. Staring, or you might even say glaring.

"Oh, great!" Dani said, and then to Pixie, "Could you wait here a minute?" Grabbing Stormy, she pushed him, squirming and sputtering, back into the kitchen.

As the door swung shut his sputtering turned into words. "What's that Frankenstein girl doing here?"

It took a while to calm Stormy down and even longer to convince him that Pixie was there as Dani's guest and if Stormy wasn't going to be polite he was just going to have to go home—immediately. She finished up by saying, "And whatever you do, don't say anything about her folks being spies, or Frankensteins, or anything like that. Okay?" And when Stormy only stared, blank-faced, she went on. "How'd you like it if people said things like that to you? About your mother?"

She thought that would get through to Stormy and she was

right. His angry glare melted into confusion and then reluctant acceptance. "Okay," he said. "I won't say it." And then added under his breath, "But I bet they are."

Dani sighed, wondering what on earth she was going to do. All by himself Stormy had been hard enough to handle, and now there were going to be two of them. Two of them almost every afternoon. She shrugged and sighed.

Obviously the very first thing she had to do was to get rid of Stormy for a minute while she warned Pixie about the kinds of things you didn't do or say around Stormy unless you wanted to risk getting your shins kicked. Thinking fast, she told Stormy to go get *White Fang,* which, fortunately, she'd put away on the highest shelf in the bedroom, where he'd have to climb up on a chair to reach it. And the minute he stomped out she rushed back to the living room, where Pixie was waiting quietly on Linda's daybed with her hands folded in her lap. Sitting quietly, but with her eyes darting around the room like charges of blue electricity.

"Does he live here?" she asked as Dani came in. "Is he your brother?"

Dani snorted. "My brother. No, he's not my brother. But he lives next door, well, at the hotel actually because his mother works there. But he comes here for me to read to him. He likes to be read to." She glanced back over her shoulder. Lowering her voice, she said, "Look, I wanted to tell you before he gets back. You gotta be careful what you say to Stormy because he has this bad temper."

Pixie nodded eagerly. "A bad temper? What does he do when—"

"Well," Dani interrupted, "he hits people. Or kicks. Actually he usually kicks." She took a deep breath. "See, it's like this. He's just fine unless somebody says something about him being a nonreader or dumb. And anything at all about his mother. He doesn't like people to even mention . . ."

But at that moment, there he was, back in the room, holding *White Fang* and still glaring. Pixie jumped up to look at the book. "Hey, *White Fang*. I've read that," she said. "It's great, isn't it? Do you like animal stories?"

Stormy stared suspiciously. Stared for a long moment before he nodded grudgingly. "Yeah," he said. "I like dog stories."

"Me too," Pixie said. "My favorite is *Lassie Come-Home*. At least that's my favorite dog story. But I like horse stories too. My favorite horse story is *King of the Wind*. Have you read *King of the Wind*?"

Stormy started to grin—tried to stop—and then quit trying. "Yeah. I—we read that one. Didn't we, Dani. I liked that one next to the best. But my best favorite book is *Doctor Dolittle*."

Pixie made a squealing noise. "Oh yes. Me too. I love *Doctor Dolittle*. And how about . . ."

Dani sat down on the daybed. For a while she stared in amazement. Then as the talk went on about what books and what parts of books were the best, she sighed and then yawned. After a while she yawned again and asked if anyone was interested in hearing the last chapter of *White Fang*.

"Yeah," Stormy said. "Dani reads good," he told Pixie. "She makes it real, like on the radio or something." He glanced at Dani, puckered his forehead thoughtfully and added, "She does when she wants to."

Dani glared and snorted. She knew what Stormy meant, and she didn't like it. Maybe once in a while she had something else on her mind, or maybe she was a little bit bored because she had read ahead and knew what was going to happen. "Humph!" she said. And then, forgetting what she'd just told Pixie about what you shouldn't say to Stormy, she went on, "You're a fine one to talk about how good somebody reads. How about if—"

But at that moment Pixie interrupted. Shoving *White Fang* into Dani's hands, she said, "Go on. Read it. I want to hear you read *White Fang*."

So Dani read, taking care to do what Stormy called "making it real." Making her voice tough and scary during the part about the escape of the evil prisoner, deep and slow when Judge Scott was talking, and higher and more fluttery for the women characters. She knew she was doing a great job by the way Stormy and Pixie listened, as if they had almost forgotten to breathe. Just as Dani was finishing the last page, Linda came in.

The next few minutes Dani was busy introducing Pixie to Linda and then explaining why she was here, and how she was going to be here every afternoon after school. Of course it was all right with Linda. But while she was telling Dani all the reasons she thought it was just wonderful that the Smithsons' little girl could visit every afternoon, Pixie and Stormy disappeared. It wasn't until Linda finally ran down and went back to the kitchen that Dani found the two of them on the front porch. As she came out the door she heard Stormy saying, "Yeah, in the graveyard. That's where Frankenstein got them."

"Stormy!" Dani practically yelled. "What are you talking about? What was he telling you, Pixie?" But before anyone could answer, the Smithson tank pulled up in front of the house and Pixie ran out to meet it.

For a few seconds Dani watched it go, watched how it slithered smoothly over bumps and potholes, before she whirled around to face Stormy. "Look," she said, hands on hips. "You promised. You said you wouldn't say anything about the Frankenstein thing. You promised!"

"Look." Stormy was imitating her, hands on hips and chin jutting. "I didn't tell her. She told me." Then he turned around and clumped off toward the hotel.

chapter

12

The next few days were pretty crazy. Piled on top of the usual end-of-the-school-year chores, such as finishing up projects and taking tests, there suddenly was a new problem to deal with. The Stormy plus Pixie problem. Not that they were fighting, or anything like that. In fact there were times when Dani almost wished they would. A fight, a good old kick-and-punch fight, would be something a person could do something about. Like telling them to stop or you'd crack their heads together. But this was different and a lot more complicated.

For example, there was the book thing. Dani had promised Stormy that, as soon as they finished *White Fang,* they'd read another dog story from the Jack London book. But she'd hardly gotten started on *Call of the Wild* when Pixie showed up with a whole armload of her own books.

"They're all my favorites," she said as she spread them out on the coffee table, running her hands over each of the books as if it were some kind of a pet animal. "I've read all of them already, but I wouldn't mind hearing them again. And Stormy will love them."

"Stormy will love them," Dani repeated, waggling her head around sarcastically. As if this three-way after-school arrangement was going to last long enough for a person to plow through—she counted six, seven, eight books. That would take at least two or three months of reading, depending on how long they were. She checked the books' widths, turning them so she could see their spines and, while she was at it, read the titles. Some of them, like *Blue Willow* and *The Five Little Peppers,* she'd never heard of before. But there were at least two that she did remember seeing a long time ago in the Sea Grove library.

"Yeah." She held up *Peter Pan* and *The Jungle Book.* "I remember both of these. They had them at my old school."

"Oh yes, they're fabulous, aren't they?" Pixie was doing her breathless little-girl voice. "Which one was your favorite?"

"Oh, I didn't read them," Dani said coolly. "I was pretty young at the time, and besides"—she spaced out the words, emphasizing each one—"I don't like to read."

"You don't?" Pixie's head was tipped to one side and she was looking at Dani in a way that definitely seemed to mean she didn't believe what she was hearing.

Dani stared back. "What's the matter?" she asked. "Don't you believe me?"

But Pixie only asked, "Why? Why don't you like to read?"

Dani shrugged. "Well, for one thing it's a waste of time. People waste their time reading when they should be doing all sorts of more important things."

"Ohhh." Pixie nodded and then frowned thoughtfully. "How come you do it then?"

Dani looked across the room, where Stormy seemed to be completely engrossed in the pictures in *The Jungle Book*. Lowering her voice, she said, "You know why. I do it to help Stormy. He needs to be read to."

Pixie lowered her voice too and asked, "Then why do you read when he's not around?"

"I don't!" Dani said, chin out and glaring. Pixie was staring back, doing her wide-eyed thing. "Well, not very often—" Dani had begun to say when Stormy interrupted.

"Yes, she does," he said. "When it gets real exciting she does. When it gets exciting she reads ahead."

Dani got to her feet and left the room. She marched through the kitchen, slammed out the back door and sat down on the back steps. Okay for you, Stormy Arigotti, she was thinking. That's all the thanks I get for reading all those boring books. Just wait until the next time you want to be read to. Just wait.

She went on sitting there for a long time, waiting for Stormy to come out to say he was sorry, but after what seemed like almost an hour she went back into the house. Crossing the kitchen quietly, she shoved the door to the living room open just a crack. Just enough to hear a deep, threatening voice saying, " ' "Am I to stand nosing into your dog's den for my fair dues? It is I, Shere Khan, who speak!" The tiger's roar filled the cave with thunder.' "

The voice was Pixie's but it definitely didn't have a breathless little-girl sound to it. Pushing the door a little farther, Dani could see that Pixie was reading from *The Jungle Book,* and, sprawled out on the daybed, Stormy had gone into his usual listening trance. When Dani let the door slam shut neither of them even seemed to notice.

That night, just to catch up, Dani read *The Jungle Book* up to where Pixie had left a bookmark. Which happened to be the place where Mowgli takes the pot of fire to the wolves' council meeting. And then she went on just a little farther, not really reading as much as skimming, to find out if Mowgli was going to be able to keep Akela from being killed by the pack. She also practiced a little, making her voice slow and sultry for Bagheera, and deep and hollow for the old bear. And the next afternoon, when she and Pixie took turns reading, she did a great job. Even Pixie said so. So after that they went on taking turns, with Dani reading one chapter and Pixie the next. Which was fine with Dani. After all, why should she care if someone else wore out their eyes and voice, for a change?

But the reading wasn't all of it. There was something else going on between Stormy and Pixie that Dani didn't like at all. Not that she was jealous, for heaven's sake. Fat chance. It was just that she overheard enough of what they were whispering to make her wonder if Stormy was talking about the Frankenstein rumor again. When she asked him he always denied it, but one time Dani was sure she heard him saying, "How did he sew the head on?" At least it certainly sounded like that was what he said. That night as soon as Pixie left for home Dani asked him about it. They were still standing out in front at the time, watching as the spooky old black car crawled off up Silver Avenue, taking Pixie home to the ranch house.

"I didn't say that," Stormy insisted. "I wasn't the one who said that." Then he cocked his head the way he always did when he was thinking, and after a while he went on, "Tell me again. How come I can't talk to Pixie about Frankenstein?"

"Because." Dani let her exasperation show in her voice. "Because it will just make her feel bad. You know. Wouldn't it make you feel bad to hear people repeating gruesome rumors about your parents? I mean, even if you knew it wasn't the truth."

Stormy nodded slowly and then asked, "What if you didn't know it wasn't the truth?"

Dani sighed angrily and demanded, "What on earth are you talking about?" But Stormy only turned around and went back into the house. When Dani followed she found him in the kitchen watching Linda peel potatoes.

It was during the last week of school that Dani found out something else that really made her mad. Something that she might not have figured out if she hadn't been looking through some of Pixie's books one night after she'd gone to bed. Just kind of skimming through them so she could decide whether Stormy might like to hear them or not. She had started looking through a boring, old-fashioned book called *The Five Little Peppers* when she suddenly remembered something Pixie had said the afternoon when she first came to visit. Something about liking the Jerky Joe cabin because it reminded her of a game she used to play. A game that came from a book *about a family with five kids.*

So that was why Pixie had found Dani's house so "fascinating." Because it was like the house in *The Five Little Peppers.* The dirt-poor little Peppers who had to use only one candle at a time and even had to pull out basting thread carefully so it could be used over again. Dani slammed the book shut and threw it across the room. Then she lay awake for a long time thinking up sarcastic questions she might ask Pixie. Questions like "How rich do you need to be to think it's fun to play a game about being poor?"

Dani didn't get around to asking about *The Five Little Peppers,* however, because another question had started to bother her more than anything else. And that was how, with Pixie around almost every afternoon, she and Stormy were going to find time to work on their running-away plans.

There had been a time, right at first, when Dani wouldn't have minded leaving Stormy out of her plans. But since he'd begun insisting on going along, and especially since she'd started dreaming about the Gila monster truck driver, she'd kind of gotten used to the idea of the two of them going together. Or she had, at least, until Pixie started complicating things.

It hadn't been easy, for instance, to find a few seconds to threaten Stormy with what would happen if they didn't start making some money. To say, "Look, we haven't had a chance to even talk about getting the ticket money lately. Because of you-know-who." She nodded to where Pixie had gone into the kitchen for a drink of water. "I can't wait any longer. So maybe we'd better just forget about you coming too."

Stormy listened, rolling his eyes thoughtfully, before he said, "But there's just two more days before school's out. And then Pixie won't come here all the time."

Dani huffed angrily. Then she said, "Yeah, well . . ." Actually she hadn't been thinking about that. How, as soon as school was out, they wouldn't be seeing so much of Pixie anymore. After she'd thought a while longer she said, "Well, okay. Till school's out. But if we don't start getting somewhere right after that, I'm going to take off by myself."

She should have thought of that. How things would be back to normal during summer vacation, when there wouldn't be any need for Pixie to spend so much time at the cabin. But then the last day of school came and went and just one day later, somebody knocked on Dani's front door at one o'clock in the afternoon—and there she was again.

"Hey," she said. "My mother had to come to town for groceries and stuff, so I came along. Would it be all right if I stayed until five again?"

And while Dani was saying, "Well, I don't know. I guess I'd better ask . . ." Pixie waved at the tank and yelled, "Okay. She says it's okay."

So that was how Pixie stopped arriving every day at the same time, and started showing up any old time at all. And that was how just a few days later, she happened to overhear a very private conversation between Dani and Stormy.

chapter

13

It happened after dinner one night when Linda had gone to see the movie at the town hall. Ordinarily Dani would have gone too but tonight it was an adults-only Greta Garbo film. So, wouldn't you know it, Dani was stuck with staying home alone and, as if that weren't bad enough, cleaning up the kitchen too.

"Me?" she'd said when Linda asked her to do it. "Why do I have to clean it? You messed it up."

Linda smiled teasingly. "Okay," she said. "Fair is fair. I promise to clean up the kitchen the next time *you* make a mess cooking dinner for the two of us. Anyway I have to leave now or I'll miss the first reel."

Obviously Linda thought her remark was pretty funny, just because Dani wasn't much of a cook. But Dani had only frowned and shrugged and went on sitting there at the kitchen table. And she was still sitting there looking at the big mess Linda had made and wishing it would just go away when Stormy slammed through the back door.

"Hi," Stormy said, looking around. "Linda went to the movie?"

Dani nodded glumly and Stormy nodded back and started wandering around the kitchen looking in all the dirty bowls and pans. After a while he said, "I'll help you clean up. Okay?"

Dani couldn't help grinning. Cleaning up a kitchen was one thing Stormy was really good at, especially the part about putting away leftovers. "Okay," she said, "go to it." And he did.

He'd just about finished the Spanish rice when it suddenly occurred to Dani that it was finally a nice, safe, private time to talk about the running-away fund. "Hey, look," she said. "If you can stop eating for a minute maybe we could have a little talk. You know, about running away. I've just about decided for certain that I'm going to leave by the end of June. So either we find a way to get enough money for two sets of tickets by then, or you'll just have to stay here."

Stormy had been scraping a big old mixing spoon around the bottom of the rice pot. *Scrape, scrape, scrape,* making Dani's scalp prickle and her teeth go all edgy. He finally quit and put the spoon in his mouth just as Dani said she was going without him. With the huge spoon still crammed into his mouth he stared, glassy-eyed, and went on staring with his eyes getting wider and glassier for so long that Dani began to wonder if the spoon was stuck to his tonsils. But finally he pulled it out and gave it a last careful lick before he said, "No! No, you can't go without me."

"Oh yeah? Who says."

"I do," Stormy said.

Dani snorted and glared. But she didn't say, "How are you going to stop me?" because she knew how. All he'd have to do is tell Linda what she was planning, like he'd already threatened to do. They went on glaring at each other for a few seconds before Stormy said, "If we could get to Reno for free, do we have enough money to get from Reno to Sea Grove?"

"I don't know," Dani said. "I'd have to figure it out. But how would we get to Reno?"

"Well, maybe like you said before. About sneaking onto the back of a truck and—"

"No!" Dani interrupted loudly, trying to shut the truck driver's monster face out of her mind. "No. I told you, I've changed my mind about that. We can't do—"

It was right at that moment that something, maybe the tiniest bit of a door squeak or the sound of breathing, made Dani whirl around, and there she was. Pixie Smithson was standing in the partly opened door looking very excited and enthusiastic. Even more enthusiastic than when she thought she was going to be chased by dead rattlesnakes. "Hi," she bubbled breathlessly, sounding, and looking, as if she were about to start bouncing off the ceiling.

Dani checked her out coolly before she said, "Hi yourself." And then cautiously, "What's up?"

"My folks went to the movie," Pixie said. "So I came here. I came here to keep you company."

"Yeah, so you came here," Dani said. "So—what's up?"

"I heard," Pixie bubbled. "I heard what you guys were talking about."

Dani sighed. "Yeah, I was afraid of that." Giving Old Bubblehead her evilest glare, she asked, "So now what? Are you going to tell?"

"Tell?" Pixie shook her head fiercely. "Oh no, I won't tell. I don't want to tell." She paused, and then, so softly Dani could barely hear, she said, "I want to come too."

Dani couldn't believe her ears. "You want to run away?"

Pixie nodded so hard her ponytail flipped up and down. "Yes. Yes, I do."

Dani checked out Stormy to see if he was as amazed as she was. He certainly seemed to be. At least he was standing there like a stone statue. A stone statue of a bushy-haired kid with a rice pot in one hand and a big spoon in the other. Dani sighed, turned back to Pixie, and asked, "Why?"

"Why?" and that was all. But for a moment her mind went on asking a bunch of other questions. Like "Why on earth would a rich kid who wears expensive clothes and rides around in a custom-built car, and who is only going to be in Rattler Springs for a few months anyway, want to go to the trouble of running away?" When she finally went on, it was in her most sarcastic tone of voice. "May I ask why *you* want to run away?"

For just a second Pixie looked uneasy, uncertain maybe, but then she nodded again and said, "Okay, I'll tell you why. But you have to tell me something first. Tell me why you and Stormy are going to run away. Okay?"

Dani said no and she really meant it. Meant that why she wanted to run away was nobody's business but her own. And Pixie agreed with her. "I know," she said. "It's none of my business. Except . . ." She paused, thought and then went on. "Except that other people who are planning to run away need to know, so they'll know whether their reasons are . . ." She paused again, looking down at her hands. "So they'll know if their reasons are good ones."

Somewhere in the midst of that long explanation, Dani lost track of Pixie's train of thought, if there'd been one in the first place. But in the meantime she'd somehow arrived in the living room and found herself sitting at one end of the daybed with Pixie at the other, and Stormy sprawled on the floor in front of them. Found herself sitting there on Linda's bed trying to put it all into words. Trying to explain about Sea Grove and how great it had been and how much she hated the town of Rattler Springs and the school and Jerky Joe's cabin, and everything. And how Linda wouldn't do anything about moving back. And then, when she'd almost finished, Stormy came out of his listening trance long enough to say, "And tell about the desert. About the desert talking to you."

At first Dani only said, "Oh that. That was just crazy stuff." But then something about the eager, excited way they both were listening made her decide to tell at least about how she'd felt that first day when she and Linda had arrived in Rattler Springs. And that got her started on how, ever since that day, she'd had this crazy feeling that she could hear the desert

101

talking to her. And the first thing she knew she'd told all of it, just like she'd told Stormy, only making it even better and more exciting. She even added a new part about how and where she'd made up her mind. How she'd been sitting in the graveyard looking at all those graves of people who had lived and died right there in Rattler Springs, when she suddenly knew she had to do it. When she finally ran down, Pixie sighed and shivered and rubbed her eyes like she'd almost been crying. She shivered again then, and turning to Stormy, asked, "And how about you? Why are you going to run away?"

Stormy looked startled. Then, as usual, he tipped his head and rolled his eyes before he said, "I don't know. I just want to. I just"—long pause—"I want to see what it looks like in Sea Grove."

Dani looked at Pixie and wiggled her eyebrows significantly. What her eyebrows were trying to say was that Stormy had some pretty good reasons even if he didn't want to talk about them. Reasons that maybe had to do with having a mother who didn't seem to like having him around, and with having to live in some crummy little rooms at the back of a run-down old hotel instead of in a real house, and stuff like that. Pixie raised her eyebrows back like she understood.

"So," Dani said. "That's our reasons for running away. Now, how about you?"

"Me?" For just a split second Pixie looked like she was trying to think what to say, or maybe decide whether she ought to say it. But then her eyes did that quick flash of fire thing, and biting her lip, she nodded slowly. "Yesss," she said, drawing it out to a sizzle. "See, it's very important that I run away soon before something terrible happens. Something unbelievably terrible." She turned to Stormy. "I think Stormy can guess why I have to run away. Can't you, Stormy? Can't you guess why I have to run away as soon as I possibly can?"

Stormy didn't answer. Instead he only did the embarrassed squirmy thing that usually meant he'd been up to no good. Dani was sure she recognized Stormy's guilty expression, but she couldn't imagine what he was guilty of that had anything to do with why Pixie had to run away. But then he said, "I didn't ask her about it. She just told me." Dani began to get the picture.

She stared at Pixie. "What did you tell Stormy?"

"Well," Pixie said. "You know that rumor about the machine my parents took up to the ranch?"

"What machine?"

"You know. The one on the big truck?"

"Yeah?" Dani had a horrible feeling that she knew what Pixie was driving at and where the conversation was headed, but she didn't intend to help it get there. She knew Pixie wanted her to ask what the machine was really for, but she wasn't going to do it. If Pixie wanted to say that her parents had a machine for making monsters out of dead people she was going to have to do it on her own, without any help from Dani. No help from Danielle O'Donnell, who didn't believe in any crazy stuff like that. Particularly crazy stuff about Frankenstein monsters. So "Yeah?" was all she had to say.

Pixie nodded, and repeated, "Yeah." The nod was slow and solemn but the blue-fire flashes were constant now. "Why do you suppose they wanted to live way out there anyway, where no one could see what they're up to? Did you ever think about that?"

"Well," Dani said. "I thought . . ." What she'd thought, what Linda had told her, was that the Smithsons were studying the rocks and soil, which had sounded pretty reasonable. After all, rocks and soil were about all there was out there. And—if they were really crazy Frankenstein scientists, where were they going to get all the body parts they were going to need? Aha! Let's see what little Miss Frankenstein says about that.

"Look," Dani said triumphantly, "maybe a house way out on the desert would be a good place to do secret stuff, but on the other hand it wouldn't be much good for getting hold of a lot of dead bodies. Where are they going to find a bunch of dead bodies way out there? Tell me that."

"Dead bodies?" Pixie asked. Then she lowered her long eyelashes so that the fiery blue light was hidden, and for a moment sat very still. When she finally looked up her eyes were wide and blank. Her voice had that childish breathless sound to it when she said, "I can't tell you. I just can't tell you about that."

Of course she couldn't, but it wasn't because it was just too awful to talk about. Or because Pixie was worried about what might happen to her if she told. Dani was pretty sure that couldn't be it. But for whatever reason, Pixie went on not being able to talk about it until the Smithson tank came up Silver Avenue and she ran out to meet it.

chapter
14

Dani didn't believe one word of it. She didn't believe that Mr. and Mrs. Smithson were planning to put a bunch of body parts together into one and zap it with a whole lot of electricity and make it come to life. Right after Pixie left she told Stormy so. "And that stuff about the body parts proves it," she told him. "Like she just didn't have time to figure out that chapter of the story yet."

But Stormy only shook his head solemnly. "She knows that chapter," he said. "She already told me about it. They're going to get them from the graveyard. She already told me they were getting some from the Rattler Springs graveyard."

Dani almost fell over laughing. "That's ridiculous. That graveyard is just an old boomtown burying place. I don't think anybody's been buried there for years and years. Not since the silver mines gave out."

"Yeah?"

"Yeah. All you have to do is read what it says on the grave markers. They're all, like, around 1900, or even before that."

"Well, what's wrong with that?" Stormy asked.

Dani was still grinning. "Well, what's wrong with that is . . . ," she said in her most sarcastic tone of voice, "what's wrong with that is, the Rattler Springs graveyard's too old. In the Frankenstein story he went to the graveyard right after someone died. Right away after, so there would be a real body, with skin and muscles and stuff like that. What kind of a monster are the Smithsons going to make out of some practically ancient bare-boned skeletons?" She was grinning when she asked, but she could tell immediately by the look on Stormy's face that he didn't see anything very funny about the idea. And after she'd had a moment to think it over, she didn't either. Nothing particularly funny about the idea of a bare-boned skeleton who'd been zapped to life, stalking around the desert looking for . . . Just like Pixie said, it was the kind of thing you didn't want to talk about. Or even think about.

She was still trying not to think about it when Linda came back from the movie and Stormy finally took himself off home. And later that night when Linda was sound asleep on the daybed couch, Dani, in her stifling hot bedroom, had something else to not think about besides Gila monster truck drivers. Rolling over for the umpteenth time, she shook her head hard to chase away a cloudy procession of monsters in greasy denims, only to have them replaced by a parade of living skeletons.

The next morning she was still thinking about what Stormy had said about the graveyard. Thinking about how ridiculous the whole thing was. She grinned, wondering what Pixie would say when she heard how old the graveyard was. But just wait, Dani told herself. When she finds out that story won't work, she'll think up a new one.

It turned out that she'd guessed right about that one. About Pixie having a better answer the next time she showed up. The only part she didn't guess was how soon that was going to be. Like early afternoon on the very next day.

When Dani opened the front door Pixie came right in without waiting to be invited. "My dad had to come in to make a phone call, so I came too," she said. "I can stay until he comes back."

"Comes back?" Dani asked.

"Yes, comes back to town. At five. Like always."

Dani looked over at the alarm clock on the daybed end table. It was just a little after two o'clock. "Well," she had just started to say when Pixie came on in and started taking some books out of a big handbag made of woven straw. "I brought some more of my books," she said. When she finished with the books she looked around and asked, "Where's Linda? I thought you said she was going to be off today."

Dani shrugged. "Yeah, I guess I did. The bookstore is closed but she took an extra job today. She's baby-sitting for the Grahams while they're in Las Vegas."

"Oh." Pixie looked around uneasily, even glancing out the

window as if she were hoping her father might still be out there so she could change her mind and go home. "Oh, I thought . . ."

She didn't finish telling what she'd been thinking, but Dani could guess. Pixie had probably figured that if Linda were home Dani wouldn't have a chance to ask any hard-to-answer questions about the Frankenstein thing. Like where you could get body parts in the desert, for instance. Maybe she hadn't come up with any good answers yet. And maybe she never would, because there just weren't any good answers. Dani was beginning to enjoy herself, watching Miss Supercool Pixie squirm a little.

"And Stormy?" Pixie asked.

Dani shook her head, trying not to look smug. "Not here," she said. "Gone somewhere on an errand for his mom's boyfriend. One of her boyfriends, anyway."

Another good try, Dani thought. Without Stormy, Miss Storyteller Smithson had lost her best audience. Sitting down in Linda's rocking chair, Dani said, "About that question I was asking when your folks showed up last night. You know, the one about where they were going to get parts for their monster? I was just wondering if you could talk about it today. And I was also wondering if you knew that the Rattler Springs graveyard hasn't been used for about fifty years. So don't bother to tell me about the graveyard."

Pixie nodded slowly. Climbing up on the daybed, she arranged herself carefully, smoothing her skirt down over her knees and crossing her feet in their scuffless saddle shoes. At last, when she was all ready, she sighed and said, "I shouldn't have told Stormy that story about the graveyard. I just did it because—because . . ." She stopped and sighed. The sigh was slow and solemn but when she glanced up Dani got a glimpse of her eyes and there was nothing slow or solemn there. "I didn't tell him the truth because it was just too— too . . ." She shuddered before she went on. "The truth is, well, my folks have this great big electric freezer. And back where they used to live there were lots of graveyards. So . . ."

Dani got the picture. And even though she certainly wasn't trying to see it, there it was, flashing before her eyes. A picture of what you might have seen in Frankenstein's freezer chest if there'd been such a thing in those days. Something cold and dead and coated with icicles and fuzzy frost. In spite of herself, a shudder crawled up her back.

"That is the most gruesome thing I ever heard of."

Pixie nodded enthusiastically. "I know." Then she sighed and her thumbnail-movie-book face flipped from eager to excited and then to sad-eyed pitiful. "And that's not the worst of it. That's not anywhere near the worst of it."

"Oh yeah?" Dani said.

"Yes. There's another part that's a lot more terrible." Pixie's voice was still gloom and doom but the quick upward flick of her eyes was something else.

"Okay. You might as well tell me." Dani sighed, trying to make her face and tone of voice say that she certainly wasn't promising to believe it, but she wasn't going to let Pixie get away with stopping at that point. "I mean, you can't say there's a worse part and just stop there."

This time Pixie's sigh was particularly long and mournful.

"No, I guess you're right." Squaring her shoulders and lifting her chin, like a person getting ready to face up to something terrible, she began, "Well, see, the other day the generator stopped for just a few minutes but then, after they got it running again I heard them talking. They didn't know I was listening but I was. And what I heard them say was . . . Well, my father said that it would have spoiled"—she paused —"er, everything if the electricity had been off much longer. And then . . ." She paused again, and when she went on her voice was like the music in a movie when it tells you something terrible is about to happen. "And then, I heard my mother say that they could still go on with the experiment if they could use parts from one other body."

Dani tried not to gulp before she asked, "Another body? Who—Whose body?"

Pixie nodded. "She didn't say. At least not exactly. But she nodded—toward my room."

Dani's gulp turned into a gasp. "Toward your room?" she repeated, sounding like a stupid parrot.

"I told you it was too terrible to talk about," Pixie said. She was looking down, hiding her eyes again. She didn't look up as she said, "But that's why I have to go with you, when you and Stormy run away."

chapter
15

That did it. It was the very next day that Pixie started being included in the running-away plans. At least more or less. Not that Dani really believed her crazy story, because she didn't. Or at least most of the time she didn't. It was only in the middle of the night, when it was easy to believe all kinds of impossible things, that she wasn't entirely sure.

Dani had gone to bed that night telling herself scornfully that Pixie sure had a big imagination. But it happened to be a dark moonless night and a black desert wind was snaking around Rattler Springs, rattling shingles and sifting sand in around doors and windows. Lying there listening to the whispering wind and crawling sand, Dani drifted off into a dream about trying to climb into a truck and being grabbed by someone who looked a lot like a Frankenstein monster except he seemed to be wearing saddle shoes and a pleated blue skirt. She woke up then and stayed awake for a long time, thinking and worrying.

The next morning, when she told Stormy about Pixie's latest tall tale, he didn't doubt any of it. Not for minute. They were in the kitchen at the time. Linda had just left for work and Stormy was at the table fixing himself a huge bowl of cornflakes. Dani had hardly finished the telling when Stormy stopped pouring milk on his cornflakes, smacked his fist down on the table and said, "Yeah. I thought so."

"You thought what?" Dani asked.

"I thought they might be going to do that."

It was a ridiculous idea. Dani tried to tell Stormy so. Tried to tell him that it just wasn't possible that parents, even slightly weird ones like the Smithsons, would ever think of chopping up their only kid. Not even if they happened to be mad scientists who needed some body parts for a Frankenstein-type experiment. "It's just too crazy," she told him. "And besides, parts from an extra-small ten-year-old just wouldn't work. Not unless they were planning to make a midget-sized monster."

But nothing she said seemed to make any difference. There just wasn't any use trying to convince Stormy that everything Pixie said wasn't the truth, the whole truth and nothing but the truth. She was still trying when Stormy interrupted by saying, "So, how soon can we leave?"

"Leave?"

"How soon can we run away? Can we do it today?"

Dani stared in amazement. "You know we can't leave yet. Not until we get some more money for tickets."

"But—But how about stowing away in a truck, like you said before?"

"What?" Dani was amazed and indignant. "I told you I changed my mind about that," she practically shouted. "So just forget about it. Okay?" She glared for a moment before she added, "Oh, I get it. So now we're suddenly in a big hurry, are we? When I was the only one who needed to get away fast, you kept slowing things down, and now suddenly we're in a big rush."

Stormy did his thoughtful eye-rolling thing for so long that Dani was getting ready to punch him before he said, "But *you* weren't about to get chopped up."

At that point Dani got up, stomped out of the house and slammed the door. She was still sitting on the back steps and Stormy was still in the kitchen eating cornflakes when a car door slammed out on Silver Avenue. Dani jumped up, dashed through the kitchen and beat Stormy to the front door. It was Pixie, of course.

Pixie came into the house on tiptoe, her fiery blue eyes darting wildly. Tiptoeing up to Dani, she whispered, "Can we talk? Is your mother gone?"

Dani backed away. "Yeah, she's gone," she said in a normal, nonwhispering voice, not wanting Pixie to think she was going along with whatever game it was she was playing now. "What's up?"

Still whispering, Pixie said, "That's what I was going to ask you. What are we going to do today? You know"—her voice got even lower—"about running away." She looked at Stormy. "Stormy told me how you were looking for a truck to stow away in."

"He what?" Dani said.

Stormy was shaking his head but Pixie didn't seem to notice. "Didn't you, Stormy?"

"No, I didn't. Not anymore I didn't." He gave Dani his guilty, squinty-eyed look. "We changed our minds about that. Now we're going to go on the bus."

Pixie looked a little disappointed. "Oh," she said, sighing. "I thought the stowaway idea sounded exciting." She sighed again, but after she glanced from Stormy to Dani and back again, she began to nod. "Oh. Okay," she said. "On the bus." Going over to the daybed, she climbed up and smoothed herself down the way she always did when she wanted to take time out. She was wearing safari-type khaki shorts and a blouse today, the kind with lots of extra straps and pockets. When she got all arranged she said to Dani, "Tell me about the bus. What's it like on a bus?"

"What's it like?" For a moment Dani thought she must be kidding, before she realized that poor little rich girl Pixie, who rode around in fancy custom-built cars, probably didn't know much about bus riding. "What's it like to ride on a bus?" she asked in a sarcastic tone of voice. "Well, for one thing you have to pay before you get on. So that's kind of the problem right now. We don't have enough money for tickets."

"Oh?" Pixie was definitely interested. "So what are we going to—?"

"We did a lemonade stand," Stormy interrupted eagerly. "We made three dollars and ninety-eight cents. But we had to stop because of Ronnie."

"Ronnie? Ronnie Grabler from school?" Pixie asked, and that really got Stormy started. He was jumping around like he always did when he told a story, but when Dani tried to stop him Pixie said, "No. Let him tell me. I want to hear about it."

So Dani went into the kitchen, dumped what was left of Stormy's cornflakes in the garbage and sat down at the table to wait until Stormy's "Gus the Hero" story was finished. But while she was waiting she began to get a new idea. The idea had to do with how adding a rich kid to their plans might actually be helpful. She was still fooling around with some new possibilities when Stormy and Pixie came into the kitchen.

Pixie was still laughing about Ronnie and the grease pit, but she stopped when Dani asked her how much money she had.

"Money? How much do I have?" Pixie asked. Fishing around in the pockets of her khaki shorts she brought out some change and started to count it. "Thirty-four, thirty-five," she said. "I have thirty-five cents."

Dani sighed. "No. I didn't mean in your pockets. I mean, don't you have some saved up at home, like in a bank or something?"

Pixie shook her head.

"How about an allowance? You have an allowance, don't you?"

Pixie thought for a moment before she shook her head again.

"You don't?" Dani made it clear she found that hard to believe.

Pixie looked thoughtful. "I did once," she said. "But they kept forgetting to give it to me and I kept forgetting to ask for it, unless I wanted something. So now I just ask when I want something, and they give it to me."

Stormy was looking excited. "Could you ask for enough for the tick—" he'd started to say when he saw that Dani was laughing. "Stop that!" he yelled. "I didn't mean tell them it was for tickets. I meant she could say—she could just say . . ."

Dani decided to come to his rescue. "Okay, okay," she said. "I know what you meant." Then she said to Pixie, "I think he means could you ask them for the money for something else, something kind of expensive, like a bicycle maybe, and then take the money and buy tickets instead?"

Pixie nodded thoughtfully. "Umm, maybe," she said. "Maybe. I could try it anyway. How much does a bicycle cost?"

Stormy was all excited. "I know. I know," he started yelling. "Wait. I'll get it. I'll go get it." He dashed away, out the back door and down the steps. *Slam, clomp, clomp, clomp, slam* and a bunch more *clomps*. For a kid who could be so quiet when he tried, it was amazing how noisy he could be when he wasn't trying.

"Where's he going?" Pixie asked. "What's he going to get?"

Dani led the way into the living room. "Who knows. Something about a bicycle, I guess."

It was a good guess. In about three minutes the slamming and clomping started all over again and Stormy burst into the room, carrying what looked like a magazine but turned out to be a bicycle catalog. A ragged, worn-out catalog full of pictures of beautiful, expensive bikes. Climbing up on the daybed beside Pixie, Stormy opened it to an illustration of a really fancy Schwinn bicycle. Someone, Stormy no doubt, had underlined and circled that particular bicycle in red and black crayon and had drawn yellow shooting stars all around it.

"See. That's it," he said. "That's a Black Phantom. It's my favorite. My favorite for a long time." He sighed, a long sad sound. "Costs too much." He pointed to where, under the picture, it said $175.00.

"A hundred and seventy-five dollars. Holy moly!" Dani said. "I didn't know a bicycle could cost that much. Linda didn't pay that much for our truck." She and Pixie looked at the picture and then at each other and then at Stormy. He was staring at the bicycle with the same kind of glassy eyes he got when he listened to a story.

Dani took the catalog away from him and slammed it down on the coffee table. "So," she said to Pixie, "I suppose if you asked your folks for a hundred and seventy-five dollars to buy a bicycle they'd say, 'Sure thing. How soon do you want it?' " She laughed, expecting Pixie to laugh too. But she didn't.

Instead she nodded solemnly. "They might," she said. "My mother used to ride bicycles and she wanted me to learn how, but mostly I live with my grandmother and where she lives there isn't any flat place to ride so I never did learn."

"You mean you don't even know how to ride a bicycle?"

Pixie nodded. "Only a little. I tried a few times on a friend's."

"And you think they might give you that kind of money to get you something you don't even know how to ride?"

Pixie tilted her head thoughtfully. "Maybe. I think so. I didn't know anything about chemistry when they bought me a very expensive chemistry set. My dad said I would learn by doing. But my grandmother took it away from me when I set the basement on fire."

Dani sighed and changed the subject to some other money-raising ideas she'd been thinking about, halfway reasonable ones like baby-sitting or dog walking.

So that was more or less the end of the bicycle conversation, and as far as Dani was concerned the end of even thinking about it. But when the Smithson tank pulled up in front of Dani's house that afternoon and Pixie ran out to meet it, she must have taken Stormy's bicycle catalog with her. At least when Stormy went home he couldn't find it. He made such a big fuss about it that Dani had to read an extra chapter of *The Jungle Book* just to calm him down.

The next day was a Thursday and Pixie didn't show up all day long. It was just about the only day she hadn't since school had been out and Stormy was really worried. He didn't exactly say so but it was obvious that he was afraid that Pixie's parents had already started collecting some body parts. Usually nothing could distract Stormy while he was listening to a story, but that afternoon he kept jumping up and running to the window every time he heard a car go by. And there wasn't any use trying to get him to think about moneymaking plans, not even for a minute.

It was fairly late in the afternoon, almost time for Linda to come home, and Dani was just about to finish a chapter when she heard the squeak of the gate hinges and then slow, unsteady footsteps on the front porch. When she opened the door there stood Pixie. Nothing else in sight. No tank-car out on the road. Just a messed-up, dirt-smeared Pixie whose face was tear-streaked—and whose hands and knees were smeared with lots of bright red blood.

"What—what happened?" Dani gasped.

Holding out her bloody hands, Pixie managed a strange, tearful smile. "I fell off my bike," she said.

chapter

16

Right at first the bike thing didn't really register with Dani. All she could think about was getting Pixie into the house and getting her hands and knees cleaned up and painted with Mercurochrome, so the skinned places wouldn't get infected. Pixie kept whimpering and trying to push Dani's hand away, and Dani kept trying to tell her it wouldn't hurt so much if she'd just hold still. So, for Dani, the bike question got put on hold for a while. Actually it was Stormy who began to get the picture first.

Stormy, who had been squatting in front of Pixie staring at her bloody knees with a horrified look on his face, made a sudden gasping noise and got to his feet. Dani looked up at him.

"Bike," he was whispering, "bike." But just then Pixie let

out a particularly pitiful moan and Dani went back to trying to be very gentle while she got the Mercurochrome on one of the worst places. She'd forgotten about Stormy until a little later, when there was a loud clattering noise, the front door flew open and Stormy came into the living room pushing a bicycle. A big shiny black bicycle with streamlined fenders, big fat tires and a very fancy paint job. It obviously was brand new, and even more obviously had cost somebody a whole lot of money.

"What? What on earth . . . ?" Dani began when Stormy said something in a strange kind of a gasping whisper. "It's a Black Phantom. A real Black Phantom. I found it in the road." He looked at Pixie accusingly. "You left it right out there in the road?"

Pixie sniffed and wiped her eyes. "I left it right where I fell off," she said. "Where I fell off the stupid thing."

But Dani's mind had gotten back on track by then and what it was telling her was really making her angry.

Getting to her feet, she stared at Pixie, hands on hips. "So!" she said. "So you said you'd ask your folks for money to buy a bicycle and we could use the money to buy tickets." Doing her sarcastic head wobble, she went on, "And then you just up and decided to ask for the bicycle instead."

"No. No, I didn't," Pixie said. "I just showed my mother the picture in Stormy's catalog and—"

"Aha!" Stormy said accusingly. "*You* took my bicycle magazine." But Pixie just nodded and went on, "—showed her the picture of the Black Phantom bike. And when I said I'd like to have one, my mother said she'd talk to my father about it.

Then she went back to the lab and I went to bed. My father had to go into Las Vegas very early this morning and by the time I got up he'd already gone. But I guess my mother gave him the catalog to take with him. So when he came back"—she shrugged and motioned toward the bicycle—"when he came back he had that with him. So then my mother came out of the lab and they gave me a riding lesson. Both of them. Both of them were out there with me for a long time."

She paused then and seemed to drift off, as if she were reliving some great experience.

"Out where?" Dani asked.

Pixie came out of her spell and said, "Where? Oh, you know, out in that parking area by the windmill. They helped me get started and then they watched me ride. But then, after I was riding really well, they went back to the lab to set up some new equipment. So I decided to ride down here and—and show you what happened." She sighed again. "Except I fell off."

"Did you hear that?" Dani asked Stormy. "Did you hear what happened to all that ticket money we could have had?"

But Stormy didn't seem to be hearing much of anything. Instead he was kneeling beside the bicycle, running his fingers over the fenders and pedals and mumbling to himself.

"Stormy!" Dani yelled. "What are you doing?"

His eyes did their squinty thing. "Looking," he said. "I'm just looking." Then he turned to Pixie. "It's a boy's bike," he said. "Why'd you tell them to get a boy's bike?"

"I told you," Pixie wailed. "I didn't tell them to get *any* kind of a bike. My father just bought one like in the picture. He probably doesn't even know about girls' bikes." Pixie shrugged and sighed. "It's not the kind of thing he notices."

It was beginning to occur to Dani that maybe, for once, Pixie was actually telling the truth. Maybe she really hadn't expected her folks to buy the bicycle instead of giving her the money. But if that was true it still left a whole lot of interesting questions. For instance—why would some mad-scientist parents who were planning to chop their kid up any day now decide to buy her such an expensive present? Dani would have asked that question and probably a few others, except that just at that moment Linda came home.

Of course Linda was all upset about Pixie's injuries. So for several minutes all that got talked about, or even looked at, was Pixie's hands and knees. Pixie had stopped sniffling and was saying that she wasn't hurting much anymore but it wasn't until Linda had examined everything and asked all sorts of questions that another problem came up. And that was how Pixie was going to get home.

"Can't she go back the way she came?" Dani asked, but Pixie was sure she couldn't.

"I'm not very good at it," Pixie told Linda. "That's why I fell off. And even if I didn't fall off again, pedaling all that way would make my knees start bleeding all over again. I know it would." She looked around. "Someone else has to do it. Someone else has to ride the bicycle out there and tell my folks to come for me in the car."

It wasn't until then that Linda began to notice the bicycle, which wasn't too surprising since Stormy had been kind of wrapped around it ever since she came in. She went over and pried Stormy away long enough to get a good look at it.

"My! It is a beautiful bicycle, isn't it?" she said to Stormy. Then she asked Dani if either she or Stormy could ride out to get someone to pick Pixie up. "Would that be all right?" she asked Pixie.

"I guess so," Pixie said. Then she whispered to Dani, "Does Stormy know how to ride a bike?"

"Oh, sure," Dani said. "He rode mine all the time till it fell apart."

"That's right," Linda said, "Stormy is a great bicycle rider. Stormy. Could you ride the new bike out to . . ."

Stormy looked up, blinking like he had just awakened from some kind of bicycle fantasy. "Could I ride the Black Phantom?" He jumped up with his eyes sparkling like crazy. "Yes, yes. I can." He turned to Pixie. "Can I? Can I ride the Black Phantom?"

Linda looked at her watch. "It's quite a long way but I think there'd be time for you to get out to the ranch before dark. And then Mr. Smithson could bring you back in the car when he comes to get Pixie."

Suddenly Stormy's eyes went wide and blank. "To the ranch?" he asked. "To where Pixie lives?" He looked scared. Frantic even. And Dani knew why. And Pixie knew why too, or at least she ought to. She was the one who had convinced Stormy that her parents were crazy Frankensteins who would just love to get their hands on a kid who was all alone way out in the desert. But Pixie didn't seem to see the problem at all.

"Yes," she said. "When you get there just knock on the door, and if they don't hear, it will be because they're both still in the lab. They probably will be." She sighed. "They both spend most of their time in that stupid place. So knock real loud and then if they still don't hear just go on in and—"

"Go . . . on . . . in . . . ," Stormy was saying between pauses that sounded like gasps. "No . . . no . . . I don't . . ."

It was then that Dani decided that she had to say something, anything to change the drift of the conversation. Because if she didn't she knew for certain that Stormy was going to blow it. He was going to say something about the Frankenstein thing right there in front of Linda. And if he did, a lot more private stuff was certain to come out.

"Hey, Stormy," Dani said. "I'll go. If you don't want to ride all the way out there by yourself, I'll go." She turned to her mother. "I guess he just doesn't want to go all that way by himself. So I can do it, Stormy. Okay?" She went over, grabbed his shoulder and shook him. "Okay?" she said again, trying to make the word say a lot of other things too. Things like "Snap out of it, kid, before you ruin everything."

"Really? Are you sure?" Linda said. "I could go over to the hotel and see if Mr. Grabler could take Pixie home in their car."

Dani was surprised. One of the few things that Dani and Linda had always agreed on was the Grabler family. Dani had heard her mother say that Howie and Brenda Grabler might not be as inclined to punch noses as their son was, but they were awfully good at sneaky stabs in the back. On the one

125

hand Dani knew that Linda hated to have to ask them for any sort of favor. But on the other, they were the only close neighbors who happened to own a car. At least, one that was in running order.

Squaring her shoulders and lifting her chin, Dani said, "No, that's all right. I can go." And a few minutes later she was out on Silver Avenue climbing onto the Black Phantom while the rest of them watched. Linda and Stormy, and even Pixie, who had managed to hobble out stiff-legged, stood on the front porch and watched as she put the kickstand up and got ready to ride. To ride out across the desert—all by herself.

chapter

17

Out on Silver Avenue, Dani turned her back on her mother and Pixie and Stormy as she got ready to ride out across the desert all the way to the ranch—all alone. As the thought began to sink in, she found herself moving more slowly. She had very carefully rolled up both legs of her jeans, had put up the kickstand and was just about to swing her right leg up over the seat when something hit her in the back, almost tipping her over on top of the bicycle. Actually, she'd been halfway expecting it—waiting for it, almost, but she wasn't about to admit that. Instead she yelled, "Stormy, you klutz. Watch it."

It was Stormy all right, hanging on to the back of her blouse and whispering in her ear, "I want to go with you. Take me along. Okay?"

"How . . . ?" she started to ask, but actually she knew the answer. The same way they'd sometimes ridden her old wreck of a bike, with one of them pedaling standing up while the other sat on the seat. So she changed the question to, "Why should I do that?" But almost immediately she knew the answer to that one too. The answer was that if you had to ride six miles out into the darkening desert it might feel a little better to have someone on the seat behind you, even if it was only a nine-year-old klutz.

Looking back at Linda and Pixie, who were still standing on the porch, Dani said, "Stormy wants to go too. Okay?"

Linda wasn't sure, at least not at first. "Won't it be harder that way?" she asked. "With all that extra weight to carry?"

That was true, of course, but after Dani pointed out that they could take turns pedaling and resting, her mother agreed it might be all right. "But you'll need to hurry along," she said, looking up at the sky. "You don't want to be out there on the bike after dark."

Dani promised to hurry, but as she turned back to the bike Stormy jerked the handlebars out of her hands. "Me first," he said. "Dibs on pedaling first." There was a moment of confusion while they figured out who should get on first before they finally got under way, weaving and wobbling their way up Silver Avenue.

The wobbling didn't last long. After the minute or two it took for Stormy to get the feel of riding the Black Phantom with a passenger on the seat, things quieted down. At least the ride did. Stormy himself was another matter. Pedaling away like crazy, he kept up a steady stream of comments about the

Black Phantom and how great it was. Things like "Smooth—smoooooth ride," and "Big old balloon tires," and "New Departure coaster brakes," and "Double-walled something or other," and "Real leather seat," and on and on and on.

After a while Dani stopped listening. Sitting on the real leather seat with her feet dangling, she held on to Stormy's belt and watched their shadow stretching out ahead of them as the desert sun sank toward the western hills. She wondered about the fact that, for the moment at least, Stormy, with his single-track mind, seemed to have forgotten all about where they were going and what they might find when they got there. Dani wished she could forget uncomfortable facts like that. Not that she believed that they were on their way to a Frankenstein-type laboratory. No way. But the truth of the matter was that nobody knew what the Smithsons were doing out there in their lonely desert hideaway. And it was impossible to know how they might feel about a couple of kids barging in and interrupting whatever it was.

And then there was—the desert. That was another thing Dani would just as soon forget about, but that, of course, was impossible. Impossible to forget where and who you were—two kids on a bicycle, a miserable little wobbly bump in the middle of hundreds of hot, dry, sinister miles. Far away from civilization, and going farther out every hot, dry, sinister minute. For a while she concentrated on trying not to think about it and that, of course, involved trying not to look at it. Which wasn't all that easy. Hard to keep from looking, for instance, at the faraway, endlessly empty horizon. Or else, nearly as bad, at the scrawny, thorny things that were making a pitiful attempt to grow beside the road. And trying hardest of all not to look up—at the endless desert sky.

With her mind so occupied with things to not think about, Dani had pretty much stopped listening to Stormy's bicycle babble, when she suddenly realized he'd stopped doing it. Not that he'd become quiet, because he hadn't. But the sounds he'd started making weren't exactly words. They were, in fact, more like puffs and groans.

"What's the matter?" she asked.

"Nothin'," he panted. "Nothin' the matter." But a minute later he was groaning again.

"You're tired," Dani said. "Let's stop. Let me pedal."

Stormy shook his head fiercely and went on pedaling faster than before. But the groans were back in a minute and before long he braked to a stop and jumped down. "Okay," he panted. "Okay. Your turn. For a little while. Just a little."

There was, Dani realized soon afterward, one real advantage to being the one doing all the work. Being the pedaler rather than the passenger meant that your mind was occupied with such things as keeping the bicycle upright in spite of Stormy's wiggly presence on the seat behind you, with avoiding potholes and washouts. And even with noticing, now and then, how "smoooooth" the Black Phantom ride actually was, at least compared to her old ten-dollar junker. And even how she needn't have bothered to roll up her pants legs because the Black Phantom's chain guard was so efficient. None of which added up to a whole lot, except for keeping her mind occupied with stuff she wasn't trying not to think about.

But six miles is a long way. Even six more or less paved and comparatively flat miles. And they were still a long way from the O'Donnell land when, dripping with sweat and gasping for air, Dani braked to a stop and let Stormy take over. They had changed places three or four times, and the cruel desert sun had finally gone down behind the western hills, when the roof of the ranch house appeared on the darkening horizon.

Dani was doing the pedaling at the time. "There it is," she told Stormy. "I can see it."

That was a mistake. "Where?" Stormy gasped, and, trying to lean out far enough to see around Dani, pulled her and the Black Phantom off balance. "Where?" he said again as the bike slowed, wobbled around desperately, and finally tipped over, dumping them both off onto the ground. Jumping to his feet, Stormy stared out across the desert with a horrified expression on his face. "Where?" he demanded again as Dani got slowly to her feet, dusted herself off and glared at him.

Grabbing his head in both hands, she turned it toward where, way up ahead, the slightly irregular horizon was broken by a short stretch of regularity. "There," she said. "That flat place. That's the roof."

"The roof," Stormy whispered. "The roof of the Frankenstein house." His eyes had gone round and wide and his mouth had too, at least until it closed in a kind of gulp. "Where they . . ." He gulped again. "Where they make the . . ."

Dani had to resist a temptation to say, "Yeah. Where they make the monsters." But she knew she'd better not. Not if she didn't want to have to drag him the rest of the way, or go on without him. Instead she only said, "Where the Smithsons

131

live. Where my mom and I lived when we first got here. And where Pixie lives now. Okay? And so now we're just going to go up there and knock on the door and ask them to come and get Pixie. Okay?"

Stormy's eyes rolled wildly and his "Okay" wobbled a little. But after he'd gulped a couple of times he said it again more firmly. "Okay. Let's go."

They walked the rest of the way. No one decided to, or even mentioned it, but for some reason no one tried to climb back on the bike. Pushing the Black Phantom between them, they moved forward slowly, watching the level spot on the horizon as it got larger and nearer in the rapidly fading light.

The ranch house Chance Gridley had built when he won all that money was a long, low building with an overhanging roof and deep verandas on two sides. It sat there all alone on the flat, open desert. All alone except for the outhouse, a couple of small shedlike barns and the well's windmill pump. Beyond it, and all around, was nothing but desert. No lawn or garden, nothing but a few dead tree stumps, all that remained of Chance's hopeless attempt to provide his ranch house with a little protection from the desert sun.

It looked, Dani decided, almost exactly the same as it had that first day when she and Linda had arrived from Sea Grove. It had been late in the day when they'd finally made it to the ranch. The sun had gone down and a red-tinged twilight was fading into darkness when their ancient truck, loaded with everything they owned, wheezed and clattered to within a few yards of the house and died a final and permanent death. And there they were—stuck in the desert hundreds of miles from home. Remembering that day, Dani shuddered.

And she shuddered again as she realized how the whole thing was repeating itself, in almost the same way. Here she was arriving again, just as darkness fell, in this awful place. A sudden feeling of panic made her come to a quick stop, almost jerking the handlebars out of Stormy's grip.

"What's the matter?" Stormy was asking and, as Dani came back to reality, she had the feeling he'd been asking over and over again. "What's the matter? Dani. What's the matter?"

Before she could stop herself Dani gasped, "I'm afraid."

Silence. A long silent pause before Stormy whispered, "Me too." Another pause and then, tugging on the bicycle, trying to turn it around, he added, "Let's go back."

Dani shook her head. Looking back over her shoulder in the direction of Rattler Springs, in the direction of six miles of rapidly darkening desert, she realized that the thought of going back through the desert night was even more terrifying, at least to her, than whatever danger might lie ahead of them.

"No," she said. "I can't." Pulling the handlebars away from Stormy, she started toward the ranch house. As she walked across the yard, pushing the bicycle, she could still hear him calling after her. A high-pitched, frightened voice, calling from a distance, "Wait. Don't. Don't go in there." But then, as she raised her hand to knock on the heavy front door, the voice came again, only this time from right behind her. "Wait for me. I'm coming too."

chapter

18

When Dani knocked on the door of the ranch house, softly at first and then more loudly, nothing happened for a long time. She knocked again, even harder, and was turning toward Stormy to say, "Maybe they're asleep," when a light appeared in the small diamond-shaped windowpane, followed by the sound of approaching footsteps. The quick, sharp footsteps came closer and closer, and the heavy door swung open.

Light poured out. Startlingly bright electric light. And standing in the midst of it, a small, thin-faced woman wearing heavy gloves and dusty coveralls. "Yes?" the woman said sharply. "What are . . ." She stopped then, and her quick, searching gaze moved to the bicycle and then out into the yard. Her voice was even sharper when she asked, "Where's Portia?"

Dani found her voice and said, "I'm Dani O'Donnell, Mrs. Smithson. Linda's daughter. What I came to tell you is about Pixie. Portia, I mean. She's at my house and—"

"Hello, Dani." Another silhouette appeared against the light beside that of Mrs. Smithson. "Portia's at your house? She's in town?" The speaker was the pale, thin-faced man Pixie had introduced as her father. "How did she get to town?"

"She rode in," Dani said quickly. "On this bike."

"What?" Mr. Smithson stared down at the bicycle and then up at Dani. It was obvious that he either didn't believe his ears, or just didn't believe Dani. "But she was here just an hour or so . . ." He stopped, pulled up his sleeve, glanced at his watch and then, turning to his wife, he went on, ". . . just a few hours ago."

"But she was only beginning to learn how to ride," the woman said. She stepped out past Dani onto the veranda, looking around as if she thought Dani was lying and Pixie was still out there somewhere in the darkness. "How could she have ridden . . ."

Dani was beginning to feel angry. "Well, she did," she said shortly. "But she fell off and skinned her knees, so . . ."

"Fell off?" Mrs. Smithson's voice was thin and quick. "Is she all right?"

"Well, she's skinned up a little. But it's not too bad. We put Mercurochrome on the skinned places. But it hurts when she bends her knees. She wants you to come in the car to get her. And we came all the way out here to tell you. On her bicycle."

"Yeah. On the Black Phantom." It was the first time Stormy had spoken since the Smithsons had made their appearance. "We rode the Black Phantom."

There was a long moment while the Smithsons looked at each other and then at Dani and Stormy. Before anyone got around to answering, Dani repeated, perhaps a little too impatiently, "We came to tell you she needs a ride. That's why we rode all the way out here."

At last Pixie's mother sighed and, turning to her husband, she said, "I guess one of us had better drive in to town right away, Ivor." She was starting to pull off her gloves as she said, "I'll go. You'll have to carry on without me." Then to Dani she said, "Come on then. Just leave the bicycle here on the veranda." She pulled some keys out of a pocket and set off toward one of the storage sheds, and Dani, after tugging Stormy loose from his grip on the Black Phantom, followed close behind her.

As soon as the weird-looking, high-wheeled automobile crept out of the storage shed with its headlights blazing, Mrs. Smithson called for Dani and Stormy to climb in beside her. To step up onto a kind of running board and from there up on to a smaller one, and then scramble into the wide front seat. When they were both in place she said, "All right. Here we go." After that, while the tanklike car slithered across the bumpy, potholed yard and then started down the only slightly less bumpy Rattler Springs road, no one said anything at all.

Dani didn't know why no one was talking. Of course

Stormy was often pretty speechless around people he didn't know very well. But, on the other hand, Dani usually wasn't. Of course it was a rather weird experience to be riding with a strange woman in an even stranger car, but that wasn't the kind of thing that usually made Dani hush up. As for Mrs. Smithson, Dani had no way of knowing if she was always so quiet. Probably not, Dani thought. But, at the moment, she did seem to have something very much on her mind.

The expression on Mrs. Smithson's face made Dani think of the out-of-it stare Linda had when she was reading a book, or maybe Stormy's when he was listening to a story. And watching Mrs. Smithson, Dani had a feeling that what she was thinking about probably wasn't Pixie and her skinned knees. And it probably wasn't about saying thank you to certain people for going to the trouble of riding all that way across the desert to let her know about her daughter's accident. Dani had almost worked herself up enough to start bringing Mrs. Smithson's attention to some of the things she might be thinking about, when the lights of Rattler Springs appeared on the horizon.

It wasn't until they were almost there that Mrs. Smithson turned to Dani and said, "I'm sorry if Ivor and I seemed a bit doubtful about your story at first. And perhaps a bit out of touch with Portia's activities. We've been particularly busy lately. That's why we thought a bicycle would be helpful, give her something challenging to do." Then with a weak smile she added, "We certainly would have noticed her absence sooner ordinarily, but this evening we were involved in . . ." She paused, and for just a moment her eyes once again had that strange gleam. ". . . involved in some especially important work, and I'm afraid the time got away from us." Her smile was tight and brief. "And, I guess it just didn't seem possible that Portia could have had time to ride all the way into Rattler Springs."

"Yeah," Dani said stiffly. "That's okay." And that was it. They had pulled to a stop in front of Dani's house and Dani and Stormy were climbing down from the high seat when Pixie hobbled out the front door. Linda had come out onto the front porch too, but Mrs. Smithson only rolled down the window, waved to her and called, "Thanks ever so much, Mrs. O'Donnell. In a bit of a hurry just now. We'll talk later."

Pixie was chattering, of course, saying good-bye and thanks, in between a lot of dramatic moans and ouches, as she climbed up onto the seat. But no one else said much of anything. It wasn't until later, when Dani and Stormy were safely back in the O'Donnells' kitchen, that the real talking began.

At first the conversation included Linda. In fact for a while it was mostly Linda because Dani's and Stormy's mouths were too full. Particularly Stormy's. Linda had made tamale pie, which was one of his favorites.

"What with all the excitement," Linda said, "and worrying about Pixie's poor little knees, it wasn't until after you'd ridden off that I realized it would be way past dinnertime before you got back."

Dani swallowed and said, "Me too. I didn't even think about being hungry until we walked in the door and smelled the tamale pie." She sighed. "I guess we had a lot of other stuff on our minds until then. Huh, Stormy?"

Stormy nodded, mumbled something and went on eating.

"It was a long way to ride, especially since you were both a bit out of practice." Linda smiled ruefully. "It must be a couple of months since your poor old bike bit the dust."

Dani held up four fingers and mumbled, "Four. Four months."

"All right, four," Linda said. "So your bicycle-riding muscles weren't in the best of shape. But you made pretty good time. You must be very tired."

More mumbling.

Linda asked some more questions about the ride and what the Smithsons had said when they heard about Pixie's injuries, but at last she must have gotten tired of the mumbled answers because she excused herself and went into the living room to read. It wasn't until then, while Stormy finished off the tamale pie, the rest of the canned peas and a couple of doughnuts, that the real talk about the ride began.

Dani finished eating, took a last sip of milk, sighed and said, "Well, the whole thing was pretty scary. Wasn't it?"

Stormy nodded hard, rolling his eyes. Stuffing the second half of a doughnut in his mouth, he chewed, swallowed and said, "Real scary. I thought we might see one. You know, right then when the door opened, I thought it might be one."

"One what?" Dani asked.

Stormy swallowed again and whispered, "A monster."

Dani covered a grin with her napkin. Shaking her head, she said she guessed she hadn't thought about that.

"You didn't?" Stormy sounded amazed. "I did. It was awful." He stared into space with unfocused eyes. "But the rest of it was okay. Riding the Black Phantom was"—he sighed—"okay." He sighed again and went on, "I thought I'd never get to. I never thought I'd even get to see one."

He got up then and went over to look in the cooking pots to see if there was anything left, and when they'd been scraped clean he started putting them in the sink. Dani went on sitting at the table, watching him and thinking about what he'd just said. He'd agreed that the ride had been scary, all right. But it obviously had scared the two of them in very different ways. Stormy had been frightened of what they might find when they got there but she herself had been afraid of . . . It took a minute to put it into words. What she had been afraid of was what might happen if for some reason they didn't get there. If for some reason they'd been stuck out there in the desert. Just thinking about it made her shudder.

Watching Stormy scrubbing pots and pans, Dani suddenly giggled, remembering how frightened he'd been when they got to the ranch house yard, and what he'd just told her about thinking a monster might come to the door. Stormy, she told herself, was a really superstitious kid. Standing out there at the edge of the open desert and refusing to walk up to the only house in miles and miles because he actually believed a monster might come to the door. That was pretty superstitious, all right. But then she stopped giggling, remembering how he'd come along when she'd started off alone.

chapter
19

By the next day the muscles in Dani's legs and back were pretty sore, and Stormy was walking strangely too.

"I'm stiff," he told Dani and Linda. "Gus said he thought I needed a grease job."

"Oh yeah, when did old Greasy Gus tell you that?" Dani asked.

"This morning, at the bar," Stormy said. "I saw him in the bar."

Linda raised her eyebrows at Dani and sighed. Dani knew what that meant. Linda didn't like the way Stormy was allowed to spend so much time in the bar. "Why were you in the bar this morning?" she asked.

"To get some money," Stormy said. "My mom gave me

money for breakfast. I got a Butterfinger and some potato chips."

Linda didn't say anything but her lips tightened as she got down the box of oatmeal and poured it into a pan. Stormy was about to get a second breakfast of good, healthy oatmeal.

When the oatmeal was gone and Linda had gone off to work, Dani and Stormy went out to sit on the front porch, where, in the early morning, there was still a little bit of shade. They were planning to sit on the steps and talk, and maybe read another chapter of *The Jungle Book*. But the talk came first and most of it was about Pixie.

"I was really mad at her right at first," Dani said. "I thought she just went ahead and got that really expensive bike with the money she'd promised us for tickets. I was so angry. Weren't . . ."

What she had started to say was, "Weren't you?" but remembering how Stormy had looked when he came into the house pushing the Black Phantom bicycle, she realized the fact that they'd just lost their ticket money probably hadn't even occurred to him. At least not at that moment.

Actually he still wasn't looking particularly angry. Worried, maybe. "Are you still mad at her?" he asked.

Dani sniffed. "Not much, I guess. Looks like she really didn't plan for it to happen that way. Like, maybe she really didn't figure her father would just up and buy her a bicycle instead of giving her the money."

Stormy looked relieved. "I guess she didn't." He bit his lip, rolled his eyes and leaned forward to look up Silver Avenue. "I wonder when she'll come back," he said.

"Huh!" Dani said indignantly. "Is that all you can think about? Well, I guess I'll just go on in then and find something better to do. And you can just—"

"No. No," Stormy said. "Don't go in. Let's read the last chapter. Let's see if Mowgli runs away."

So Dani started to read but it was a long chapter and she noticed that Stormy wasn't really into it, the way he usually was when he was being read to. Every once in a while she caught him leaning out to look past her up Silver Avenue. For some reason it bothered her a lot.

"Okay," she said finally, when she caught him staring up the road for about the umpteenth time, "what did I just read? I'll bet you weren't even listening."

"I was," he said. "I was too. Mowgli and the wolf were talking about the tiger. But I was just looking . . ."

"Yeah? What were you looking for?"

Stormy did his guilty, squinty-eyed thing. "For the Black Phantom," he confessed. "I was looking to see if she's going to come on the Black Phantom."

So Dani told him he could just go on out to the road then, and wait for his beloved Phantom. Or he could settle down and listen. But not both.

After that Stormy did stop looking, but Dani thought he was still listening because his ears seemed to be quivering. Sometimes in the past when she'd been reading a really exciting part Dani had thought she could see his ears quivering, but this time she wasn't sure if his ears were tuned in to the story or to the whirr of bicycle wheels. It wasn't until Shere Khan was about to be trampled to death by the buffalo that,

143

for a little while at least, they both forgot about Pixie and the Black Phantom and started concentrating on the story.

It was a good thing they forgot too, because Pixie didn't show up at all that day. And not the next day either. For those two days Stormy was at Dani's house even more than ever, doing all his usual things. Things such as eating and bugging Dani to read to him. All his usual activities with a few more or less unusual ones thrown in for good measure—like running to the front window every few minutes and asking Dani over and over again if she thought Pixie was all right.

"Sure, she's all right," Dani kept telling him. "Why wouldn't she be?" She went on, using her most sarcastic tone of voice. "If a person could die from skinned knees I'd have been dead years ago."

"No. It's not that."

Dani frowned and shook her head disbelievingly. "You're not still worrying about her folks chopping her up, are you?"

Stormy looked embarrassed. "No," he said. "Course not." But Dani didn't know if she believed him.

"Look," she told him. "Forget all that Frankenstein stuff. Okay? I mean, you saw her parents. Both of them. And they didn't look anything like crazy scientists, did they?"

Stormy shook his head thoughtfully. "Nooo," he said, dragging the word out in an uncertain way. "Not crazy, I guess. But strange. They did look kind of strange."

Dani thought of saying that a lot of people had strange parents and that didn't mean they were about to get chopped up into monster parts. But instead she just shrugged and changed the subject.

Pixie didn't show up at all the rest of that day either, but when Linda came home from work she had news. She said that Pixie was fine and that she would be visiting tomorrow. All day tomorrow. "Mr. Smithson stopped by the bookstore this afternoon," Linda said, "to ask if it would be all right if Portia spent the day with us tomorrow while he and Mrs. Smithson were away. He said her knees were healing up nicely, and they wanted to thank you for doing such a good job with the Mercurochrome."

Dani gave Stormy a "See, what did I tell you" look, but he ignored her. "Did he say anything about the—Black Phantom?" he asked.

"The Black . . . ," Linda started to ask before her question turned into, "Ohhh. You mean the bicycle. As a matter of fact Mr. Smithson did mention the bicycle. He asked if it would be all right if Portia brought it with her when she comes tomorrow."

Stormy lit up like a Las Vegas casino. "Will it?" he asked. "Did you say it would be all right?" And when Linda said she'd told Mr. Smithson it would be, he ran around the room a couple of times, and then said he was going home and go to bed early, so morning would come faster.

Things were different that evening with no Stormy hanging around, and one of the differences was a long talk Dani had with Linda.

It started when Dani came into the living room to look for a book of puzzles and noticed that her mother, who had been curled up on the daybed, was acting kind of strange. The first strange thing she did was to turn her face away when Dani came in. And then, while Dani was squatting in front of the bookcase, there was a sniffing noise, and when she turned around quickly, Linda was wiping her eyes.

Right at first Dani just went on looking through the shelves, pretending she hadn't seen anything, but she couldn't help wondering. She couldn't remember seeing her mother cry before, at least not very much. Perhaps she'd cried a little, way back when they heard that Chance had died, and maybe some angry tears once when the Grablers had refused to mend the cabin's leaky roof and then raised the rent. But those were the only times Dani could remember. More often, when she'd worried about her mother, it was just the other way around. Like worrying how she could go around being so cheerful when there was absolutely nothing to be cheerful about.

Dani decided she would pretend she hadn't noticed. She found the puzzle book and started to leave the room when all of a sudden, without even deciding to, she found herself saying, "What's the matter?"

Right at first Linda insisted that nothing was. "I'm just feeling a little down today," she said. "It's the heat, I guess." But when Dani went on staring at her she sighed shakily and said she was worried about her job with Mr. Cooley. "He's thinking of selling the bookstore," she said with a strange catch in her voice. "He's probably going to move to Arizona to live with his daughter. And if he does, there goes my job. And just when I was hoping we could get in better shape financially, now that we have the rent money from the ranch and all." She sniffed again and wiped her eyes before she sighed and said, "And now just today, when I was in the market I saw Brenda and she said she and Howie might have to raise the rent again."

So then Dani said in what she hoped was a "well, then, that's settled" tone of voice, "Well then, it sounds to me like it's the perfect time for us to pack up and go back to Sea Grove." But that just got them started on the same old argument they'd had so many times before. Linda started the way she always did by saying, "But we can't just go off and leave a bunch of debts here in Rattler Springs." She sighed again. "Just a few more months with the extra money for the ranch, and I could have paid everything off. But now . . ." She waved her hands in a shaky "who knows" gesture. "Without a truck, or even a car, we'd have to leave everything behind. And how could we manage in Sea Grove with no money and no place to live and not even any furniture?"

Dani had heard it all before and as far as she was concerned none of it made much of a difference. She was sure that once they got to Sea Grove, Heather's family would let them visit for a while. And Linda would be able to get a good job and people would let them charge things until they got settled. The important thing was for them to get out of the desert.

So the argument went around and around in the same old way, the only difference being that this time Linda complicated everything by crying. Dani wished she could cry too just to even things up, but for some reason she couldn't. She just didn't seem to be the crying type.

It didn't seem fair. None of it seemed fair. After a while Dani got so frustrated that she slammed out of the house. Out on Silver Avenue she stopped for a moment to consider where to go. Not out across the desert toward the graveyard. Not now when the reddish twilight was already fading away toward darkness. Instead she would go down to the General Store and maybe do a little shopping. Fishing in her pocket, she found a nickel and two pennies. Well, maybe not much actual shopping, but a little "just looking" would give her something to do while she calmed down, and while Linda had time to start wondering where she had gone.

Walking against a grating, sandy wind, she reached the corner and turned down past the Grand Hotel's bar, where bright lights and loud music were still spilling out of the open door. But a few yards farther on the General Store was closed and dark. She hadn't realized how late it was.

She went on then, past the post office, but just as she turned to take the path that led back through the vacant lot, something made her look back toward Gus's place. And there it was. Silhouetted by a dim glow that oozed out through the gas station's greasy windows, a beat-up old truck was parked at an angle, its large, lumpy load covered by a flapping tarp. Dani whirled and ran for home.

Later that night, lying in bed in her stuffy room, with the window tightly shut against the blowing sand, Dani pounded her pillow in frustration. Everything, it seemed, was falling apart at once. Pixie's offer to provide ticket money by asking for a bike, Stormy's interest in the running-away plan, and now maybe even Linda's job at the bookstore. Everything seemed to be slipping away.

And there was something else that seemed to be slipping away too. Something important that she couldn't quite put her finger on, but what it felt like was a kind of—certainty. A conviction that she'd had ever since that day in the old grave-yard when she'd decided she really was going to run away. But she wasn't going to let that happen. Grabbing her pillow with both hands, she held on tightly, telling herself over and over again that she was going to leave before—before the end of June. She held on to that idea and the edge of the pillow until she went to sleep.

chapter

20

It was early the next day, barely daylight actually, when the Smithsons' car pulled up in front of the O'Donnells' cabin and unloaded Pixie and the Black Phantom. Stormy, who'd arrived early too, went to the door with Dani. Even though they were right there as Mr. Smithson pushed the Black Phantom up onto the porch, he didn't have much to say to them. Just a hurried hello and good-bye before he turned back to where Mrs. Smithson was waiting in the car. Strangely silent as always—both of them.

But Pixie was the same as always too, except, of course, for some pretty spectacular scabs on her hands and knees. Bouncing into the living room, she jabbered away about what a good bicycle rider she was turning out to be, and how she'd been wearing some special knee pads that belonged to her mother, in case she fell off again.

"Knee pads?" Stormy asked. And when Pixie just went on jabbering about the bicycle, he asked again, "Your mother wears knee pads?"

"Yes, you know, for digging. She wears them for digging," Pixie answered, and went right on about how fast she could start and stop, etc., etc. She didn't seem to notice the anxious look on Stormy's face but Dani did. She had already figured out what was worrying him when he poked Pixie and asked, "Where? Where does your mother dig?"

He went on asking "where" but before he got Pixie's attention Linda came in and Pixie started talking to her. Stormy shut up then, but he hadn't forgotten because when Pixie followed Linda into the kitchen he started in on Dani. "Those knee pads. For digging." He nodded with an "I told you so" expression on his face. "In graveyards, I betcha."

Dani snorted. "Don't be silly," she said. "People wear knee pads for all sorts of digging. Like in gardens, for instance."

"Gardens?" Stormy sounded like he'd never heard the word before.

"Yeah, gardens." Dani shrugged, admitting to herself that it wasn't a word you heard much around Rattler Springs. "Or when you're digging up minerals and like that. You know, like geologists do. *Geologists,*" she repeated significantly. "Like what the Smithsons are."

Stormy nodded but he didn't seem convinced. However, he quit worrying about knee pads as soon as they went back out to look at the Black Phantom, even though they were right there hanging over the handlebars. Staring at the shiny black bicycle, Stormy's eyes had the same glassy look they got in the midst of a good story.

Dani had been planning to have another ticket-money conference with Stormy and Pixie as soon as Linda left for the bookstore, but the way it turned out there wasn't much time. Stormy wasn't in the cabin very much that morning. Instead he spent most of it riding up and down Silver Avenue in the blazing sunshine. Except now and then when Pixie insisted on having a turn. And even then it was impossible to talk to Stormy, unless you wanted to talk about bicycles.

It was after his second or third turn, while he waited on the porch for the next one, that Dani stuck her head out the door and said, "Look, are you guys going to ride that thing all day or can we save out some time for a little talk?"

"Talk?" Stormy said blankly, as if he hadn't the slightest idea what they might have to talk about.

"Yeah, a talk." Dani looked around and lowered her voice even though Linda was long gone and no one else was around. "About the ticket money. We're going to have to do something in a hurry, now that the bike money . . ." She paused and then added with special emphasis, "Now that the bike money got wasted."

Stormy looked at her blankly for a moment before he got the point. "Not wasted," he said. "The Black Phantom's not wasted." Cocking his head, he looked at Dani thoughtfully before he added, "You can ride too. You want a turn?"

Dani felt like yelling, "No! Riding a stupid bicycle in a

hundred-degree temperature is not what I've been waiting for all my life." Instead she put her hands on her hips and said, "For your information, Mr. Arigotti, in case you've forgotten everything we were talking about, the only thing I want is some *money* for bus tickets."

Stormy wiped his sweaty face with the back of one hand. "Oh yeah," he said, "money. For tickets." And then after a second, "Pixie has some money. I saw it. She has a lot of money."

Dani had started asking questions like "She has?" and "How much does she have?" and Stormy was still doing his slow-motion concentration thing when Pixie came back down Silver Avenue and braked to a sliding stop outside the gate.

"Hi," she said as she jumped off the bike and kicked down the stand. "Did you see that? Did you see me burn rubber?"

"Yeah, we saw you," Dani said. "Stormy says you have some more money. Why didn't you tell me about it?"

"Money?" Pixie looked puzzled for a moment before she said, "Oh yes, for lunch. I have some lunch money." She reached in her pocket and pulled out a ten-dollar bill. "My father gave me this for lunch. I'm supposed to take you and Stormy to lunch because you're letting me stay all day. I'm supposed to take you to the Silver Grill. Your mother too, if she can leave the bookstore."

"Wow!" Stormy said. "Wow!"

Dani didn't say "wow" but she halfway thought it. While ten dollars wasn't nearly enough to buy three sets of tickets to Sea Grove, it would do a lot in that direction. For just a moment Dani thought about trying to convince Pixie to forget about Silver Grill lunches and settle for peanut butter sandwiches at home. But that seemed pretty risky. For one thing it wouldn't be easy to convince Stormy, and besides, Pixie's parents might ask Linda if she enjoyed the lunch. One way or another, the truth was likely to come out.

"Oh yeah? The Silver Grill?" Dani said nonchalantly, but loudly enough to drown out Stormy's comments.

"Yes," Pixie said. "I guess we can have whatever's left over for ticket money. My father won't remember to ask for it back. He never does."

Dani shrugged. "Well, that's better than nothing," she said. "It's not as much as a Black Phantom bike, but it's better than nothing."

Pixie's changeable face went from happy to tragic in a flash. Hanging her head, she said, "I know. I should have told them I wanted to shop for the bicycle myself, but I just didn't think about it. But I should have guessed he might do something like that. My father is always doing weird things. It's just that he usually doesn't think very much about what he's doing, because he's so busy thinking about other stuff while he's doing it." She stopped then and sighed.

"What other stuff?" Stormy asked quickly.

"Oh, stuff like . . . ," Pixie started to say but then, after checking out Stormy's anxious face, she went on more slowly, "Oh, stuff like what they're working on. You know, in the laboratory?"

Stormy's eyes widened. "Stuff?" he asked. "What stuff in the laboratory?" But instead of answering him Pixie just looked at her wristwatch and made a little squealing noise. "Hey," she said. "It's lunchtime. Come on. Let's go have lunch."

That did it. If there was one magic word that would get Stormy's mind off Frankenstein monsters it had to be *lunch*. So a few minutes later all four of them, including Linda, were sitting around a table in the best restaurant in Rattler Springs. The absolute best, which, as Dani mentioned, wasn't saying much since its only competition was the lunch counter at the back of the Grablers' General Store.

There weren't that many choices on the menu. Linda ordered chicken soup and a salad but everyone else wound up with hamburger steak sandwiches with French fries. For dessert they all ordered chocolate sundaes. But even though the food wasn't terribly exciting, it was a little better than peanut butter sandwiches, and for a while the whole eating out thing was kind of okay.

Linda told some stories about the bookstore that Dani had heard before, like how prissy old Mrs. Alwood checked out self-improvement books and then snuck out with *True Romance* magazines hidden under her purse. Linda kind of acted out the stories the way she did sometimes, and Stormy and Pixie laughed like crazy. Watching them, it occurred to Dani that they probably thought that having a mother like Linda would be a lot of fun, a thought that for some reason made Dani angry, particularly after she remembered that she used to feel pretty much the same way, when she was their age.

The giggling was still going on when the Silver Grill's front door banged open and Ronnie Grabler came in. After stopping for a moment to look around, he swaggered across the room, heading right for their table.

Ignoring the rest of them, he looked right at Linda and said, "Hey, where you been? I been looking for you."

"For me?" Linda looked worried, which certainly wasn't surprising. Hearing that a Grabler was looking for you, even if it was only old Ronnie, would worry just about anybody. What was surprising to Dani was her own reaction, which felt a lot like anger. Throat-squeezing, heart-pounding anger.

She'd had enough experience with anger attacks to know that when you're in the midst of one, your thoughts can get a little confused. But what she was thinking at the moment seemed perfectly calm and logical. What she was thinking was, Where does a stupid overgrown kid get off telling somebody's mother that he's looking for her? She was just about to say so out loud when Ronnie said, "My dad wants to see you. He said to tell you he wants you to come by when you get off work today. He wants to see you today." He didn't go on to say, "And you better be there," but his tone of voice made it pretty clear that was what he meant. Then he swiveled around on the high heels of his cowboy boots and strutted off.

From then on the lunch definitely went downhill. When Linda left for the bookstore, she was still looking upset and worried, and Dani went back to the cabin feeling pretty much the same way. Pixie and Stormy didn't seem too concerned right at that moment, but a little later, during Stormy's first turn on the bike, Pixie came into the house looking for Dani.

"Hi?" she said, making the word sound like a question. A question like "Are you okay?"

Dani, who'd been lying on the daybed on her stomach, with her chin resting on her folded arms, raised her head and said, "Yeah, yeah, I'm okay." And then, after a pause, "I guess I am."

Pixie came closer. "I don't think so," she said.

"What don't you think?"

"That you're okay. You don't seem okay to me."

Dani shrugged. "Okay, so I'm not okay."

Pixie stared at her for a moment before she said, "I have some money for our running-away fund." Fishing around in her pocket, she brought out three dollar bills and some change. "There," she said. "It's three dollars and eighteen cents. It's not enough, I know, but I'm going to get some more. On my birthday. I always get lots of money on my birthday."

"Oh yeah? When's that?" Dani asked.

"Next week," Pixie said. "On June twenty-fifth."

"Yeah, well, that's great. But you aren't really going to get enough for the tickets, are you? I think we'll need almost fifty dollars more if we're all going to go."

Pixie nodded thoughtfully. "I think I'll get more than that. You know, from my grandmother."

Dani sighed inwardly. Pixie looked and sounded so confident—and honest. It was hard not to believe her, even though you knew you'd better not.

"That much?" Dani asked.

"I think so." Pixie nodded again and sat down on the other end of the daybed, folding her hands in her lap. After a minute she asked, "What else?"

"What do you mean, what else?"

"What else is wrong?"

Dani thought about saying, "Nothing. Nothing else." After that she considered, "None of your business," but instead she wound up telling the truth. "I don't know what else is wrong, but something always is when the Grablers want to see you." She took a deep breath before she added, "I just have this feeling that something very bad is about to happen."

chapter

21

It wasn't the first time that Dani had had a premonition that something awful was about to happen, and her premonitions had usually come true. Although on second thought, she had to admit that the awful thing that happened sometimes wasn't all that easy to spot. There had been, for instance, occasions when it had taken a while before she recognized as pretty awful some event she might have failed to notice if she hadn't been looking for trouble.

But the premonition she had that afternoon while Linda was visiting the Grablers was the strongest one ever, and what it was telling her was that something terrible was about to happen. When Linda finally showed up, though, it seemed that just the opposite was true. At least it did right at first.

It was late when Linda finally appeared. The black tank had

159

long since crawled to a stop outside the cabin door, and Pixie had run out to meet it. Even though dinnertime had come and gone Stormy was still right there in the O'Donnells' kitchen, looking hopeful. At last Dani decided somebody had to do something, so she began to peel some potatoes. She was starting on the second one when Linda finally walked slowly up the back steps and into the kitchen, looking—not angry exactly, but not happy either. Just tired and worried.

"So what happened? What did they want?" Dani demanded immediately. "What did the Grabby Grablers want to see you about?"

Linda put her purse down on the table and stood for a second or two with her back to Dani before she turned around slowly and said, "It seems the Grablers want to buy our ranch. They made an offer for all of it. The house and the land too."

Trying to control a surge of hope and excitement that for a moment almost swamped her voice, Dani said, "But why? I mean, why do they want to buy it? When we were trying to sell it before, they said it was worthless." Dani remembered very well what the Grablers had said, which was that the O'Donnells' land was worse than worthless because the upkeep and taxes would be more than what you could sell it for.

Linda nodded. "I know. I don't understand why they've changed their mind." Sitting down at the table, she stared off into space for several seconds before she went on. "Brenda tried to make it sound as if they were doing it out of the goodness of their hearts, because they'd heard I might be losing my job. But I found that a little hard to believe." She smiled ruefully. "However, it's true that whatever their moti-

160

vation was, there didn't seem to be much of it. Judging by what they were offering, at least."

But at that point Dani wasn't concerned about offers and motivations. The rising tide of hope was getting higher and higher. Putting down the half-peeled potato, she sat at the table opposite her mother. "Well, what I think," she said, her voice a little jittery with excitement, "is that you ought to take it. I mean even if it's not very much it's got to be enough to pay off our debts and move us back to Sea Grove. It has to be that much, doesn't it?"

Out of the corner of her eye Dani noticed that Stormy had taken her place at the sink and was finishing the potato she'd been working on. A move which she should have questioned since Stormy often had bad luck with sharp objects. But her mind was elsewhere. "It has to be that much, doesn't it?" she asked her mother again.

Linda sighed. "That's just it. It isn't that much. What they're offering is ridiculous, really. They're willing to honor my lease to the Smithsons for five more months and pay me three hundred dollars besides, if they can buy the property immediately. Which means they'd get the house and all that land for just three hundred dollars of their own money." She shook her head slowly. "It would pay off our debts, just barely, but with hardly anything left over. It's really an unbelievably low offer."

"But we have to take it," Dani wailed. "It's probably the best chance we'll ever have to get out of here. We have to take it."

But Linda only shook her head, and it was then that the

premonition about something terrible happening began to come true. This time it turned out to be the worst argument that Dani and her mother had ever had. The argument went on and on, with both of them saying the same old things, only getting angrier and meaner than usual. After a while they were practically shouting at each other.

At one point Dani yelled, "You just don't care about what I want or what happens to me. You wouldn't care if I just dried up and blew away, would you? Then you could just go on reading your mushy books and listening to your soap operas without anyone bugging you all the time. That's right, isn't it?"

And then Linda said, "No that's not true, Danielle O'Donnell, and you know it. You know I want to leave here too, but there's no way we can do that when we have nowhere to go and no money to get there."

There was no telling how and when the argument might have ended except that just as the shouting was at its worst Stormy started yelling too. But what he was shouting was, "Ow, ow. I'm bleeding to death."

Of course Stormy wasn't bleeding to death, but it was a pretty deep cut, and everything else came to a stop while Linda ran to get her first-aid things and then worked at getting the bleeding to stop. By the time she was finished with the bandaging, Stormy had stopped worrying about his finger and had started worrying about the potatoes. "Did I bleed on the potatoes?" he kept asking. "Can you eat bloody potatoes?"

It was just about then that Linda got very stubborn and insisted that there would be no more discussion about selling or moving until dinner was over. "Absolutely none at all," she said. "Do you hear me, Dani?" It sounded like she really meant it, and it turned out she did, because when Dani tried to sneak in one more important point her mother put down what she was working on and said she was going to throw the dinner in the garbage and go lock herself in the bathroom if Dani didn't shut up.

Being told to shut up was something that Dani wasn't used to, and it made her really angry. For a second she actually thought about saying, "Go ahead and do it." But then she happened to look at Stormy. It was the horror-struck expression on Stormy's face, along with the fact that by then she herself was pretty hungry too, that made her bite her tongue. But as soon as dinner was over and Stormy had gone back to the hotel the argument started up again.

Linda was still sitting at the table finishing her cup of tea and Dani sat down too. Trying to keep her voice calm and reasonable, she said, "Anyway, you didn't tell them no, for sure, did you?"

Linda shook her head. "No, not exactly," she said. "I said I'd need a while to think about it."

So there was still some hope. Keeping her voice as calm as possible, Dani said, "Okay, then just promise me one thing. Just promise me that you won't tell them no, for sure, until we have time to talk about it some more."

But then Linda said she didn't think she could wait very long to decide. "They really seem to be in a hurry," she said. "When I reminded them that the ranch was leased to the Smithsons for almost five more months, they said that was all right but the sale had to go through right away or they wouldn't be interested."

"That's crazy," Dani said. "If they're in such a hurry to buy the house, why don't they care if someone else has the right to go on living there for such a long time?"

"That's right," Linda said. "It does seem strange. In fact it seems to me that there are just too many suspicious things about this whole offer."

That didn't sound good. "But you won't say no right away, will you?" Dani pleaded.

Linda sighed and shook her head. "Dani," she said. "I promised them I'd give them an answer by Thursday. And I'm afraid the answer will have to be no."

At that point Dani slapped both her hands down on the table and jumped up so fast her chair fell over backward. As it crashed to the floor she ran from the room, pausing only long enough to shout, "You'll be sorry. If you make us stay here forever you're really going to be sorry."

chapter

22

It was that very night, the night of the big fight with her
mother, that the feeling of certainty came back. It was then
that the absolute certainty that she, Dani O'Donnell, was
about to leave Rattler Springs returned with all the strength it
had that day in April, in the old graveyard.

Sitting cross-legged on her bed—much too hot and angry
to even think of going to sleep—Dani thought for quite a
while about the reasons she'd almost lost her determination.
Part of it was Stormy's fault, of course. His fault at first for
insisting that he was going with her and then, after she'd
gotten used to the idea and begun to depend on it, losing
interest in the whole project. She didn't know why Stormy
had finked out, but it wasn't hard to figure that Pixie's arrival

on the scene had something to do with it. Pixie and, of course, the Black Phantom.

It really made Dani angry when she thought about Stormy turning into such a two-faced traitor after she had been his best, almost his only, friend for such a long time. And after all those hours of reading out loud, too, not to mention all those healthy meals. Of course she had to give Linda some of the credit for the meals, but if Dani hadn't been letting the little pest hang around he wouldn't have been there to be fed all that healthy stuff. And then, after all that, for him to throw her over for a lousy little liar and her expensive bicycle.

And speaking of the little liar, Pixie herself was also to blame for Dani's feelings of discouragement. No one but Pixie could have caused the hopeless feeling that happens when something terribly important is promised to you and then, at the last moment, snatched away. As when you were promised one hundred and seventy-five dollars for the running-away fund and then, at the last moment, discovered that all that money had been spent on one stupid bicycle.

So losing that wonderful fierce certainty had been partly Stormy's fault and partly Pixie's—and, an even larger part, Linda's. Like maybe Linda had guessed what Dani was planning to do and, instead of saying so, had tried to stop it by being pitiful.

Like that day she'd cried about losing her job, for instance. Dani had felt that those tears were definitely unfair. And the other things that Linda had been doing to make Dani feel guilty weren't fair either. But she wasn't going to feel guilty anymore. All that guilty stuff had ended when Linda decided to turn down the Grablers' offer and threw away the best chance she and Dani would ever have to get back home. She would never, Dani told herself, forgive her mother for that. In fact she probably would never speak to her mother, ever again.

Picking up her pillow, Dani punched it hard, and the punch felt strong and certain, and the next morning she woke up feeling the same way. Hard and strong, and certain that she was going to run away very soon. Maybe Stormy and Pixie would be going too and maybe they wouldn't, but it didn't matter a bit one way or the other. Dani O'Donnell was definitely going to leave Rattler Springs for good and always, before that very week was over.

Getting out the beat-up old envelope from the back of her underwear drawer, Dani counted the money in the running-away fund. There was now, with the addition of the three dollars and eighteen cents left over from the cafe lunch, a total of forty dollars and twenty-five cents. Which would probably be just about enough for one person to get all the way to Sea Grove, if the one person didn't spend much on anything else. Like food, for instance. Dani smiled grimly. All right, she'd go without food. Unlike some other people she knew, she didn't consider stuffing her face the most important thing in life. Being careful to keep her jaw at a firmly determined angle, Dani got dressed and went to the kitchen to have breakfast.

It was late, but to Dani's surprise Linda was still there, rinsing out a coffee cup at the sink. No sign of Stormy, though, which was another surprise. Right at first, when Linda said good morning, Dani just nodded, keeping her jaw set, even after she noticed the big platter of apple pancakes, her favorite breakfast. But after a moment she began to reconsider her decision to never speak to her mother again.

Not that she was any less angry. And certainly not that the apple pancakes made any difference. It was just that it suddenly occurred to her that, right at the moment, any sort of out-of-the-ordinary behavior might not be a good idea. For instance, anything that might make a certain person feel that she had to be especially watchful for the next few days.

So Dani forced herself to smile a little the next time her mother looked at her and then, just before Linda left the house, she even went so far as to mention that the apple pancakes were very good. Linda said, "I'm so glad," in a surprised tone of voice and, as she left for work, she patted Dani on the shoulder. At the door she stopped once to say that she was going to try to get home from the bookshop a little early, and another time to ask, "Where do you suppose Stormy is? I made enough pancakes for him."

Dani shrugged. "Yeah," she said. "I noticed."

Linda went out then, and a few minutes later Dani left too, on her way to the bus stop. Of course no bus ever arrived in Rattler Springs that early in the morning, and there were no buses at all on Wednesdays, but that didn't matter. All she was planning to do at the moment was to check the most recent bus schedule, and perhaps ask Rosie Arlen, the post office/bus station operator, a few important questions. Questions like what time the Thursday bus usually got into Rattler Springs and, just in case Pixie or Stormy might be going too, at what age a person had to start paying the full adult fare.

Mrs. Arlen, sometimes known as Nosey Rosie, had sold bus

tickets as well as stamps for as long as Dani could remember. She was a large, round woman with several double chins and eyebrows that were plucked out and penciled in. Everybody said she knew everything about everybody in Rattler Springs, and what she didn't know she was determined to find out one way or another. But Dani wasn't too worried. Nosey Rosie could be pretty sneaky, all right, but so could Dani O'Donnell.

She began by looking around the post office. At the public notices and wanted posters and things like that, as if she were just killing time without having anything particular in mind. She looked at the bus schedule notice too, but she knew better than to take what it said as the final word. She'd lived in Rattler Springs long enough to know that buses seldom arrived there on time. When she finally strolled over to the counter the first thing she asked was whether the Thursday bus from Las Vegas had been getting in on time recently.

"Oh my, no," Mrs. Arlen said. "Not recently. They're supposed to be here between five and six in the afternoon but in this kind of weather they usually have to stop along the road to keep from overheating. Lately they've been getting in pretty much any time from five to midnight."

"Oh," Dani said. "I was just wondering." She started to leave then, or pretended to, before she turned back and asked, "Do nine-year-olds have to pay the full adult fare?"

Mrs. Arlen narrowed her eyes and said, "No, my dear, nine-year-olds don't pay adult fare." She leaned forward then and, arching her penciled-in eyebrows, she added, "But we both know you're a bit older than that. Don't we, missy?"

Dani thought about asking if she also knew that people with fat faces oughtn't to wear skinny eyebrows, but she didn't. Instead she only unclenched her teeth enough to say she knew she was too old for a children's ticket but that she was just asking for a friend. She left then and headed back toward the cabin, but as she was going past the Grand Hotel she ran into another of Rattler Springs' charming residents, Ronnie Grabler.

Ronnie, who had been leaning against one of the posts that held up the Grablers' private awning, stepped out into the middle of the sidewalk and put out an arm to block her path.

"So?" Dani said, giving him her coldest stare. "What do you want?"

Ronnie's grin was just as sinister as always. "Guess you heard the news already," he said.

"What news is that?" Dani asked.

"The news that my folks are going to buy your mother's ranch."

"Is that what you heard?" Dani asked. And then, to her own surprise and shock, she heard herself adding, "What I heard was that your folks' offer was ridiculous and my mom's going to turn it down."

"Oh yeah?" Ronnie's pudgy face twisted into a bulldog snarl. "And what I heard was that if your mom does that, my folks are going to raise the rent on a certain old cabin." He chuckled evilly. "I mean, you folks can't expect to live in a famous place like that for peanuts. So what I heard is my folks are going to raise that there rent a whole lot. That's what I heard."

"Is that so?" Dani could feel a hot, red tide of anger oozing across her face. "Sounds like a Grabler trick, all right. Folks don't call you guys the Grabby Grablers for nothing." It wasn't a very smart thing to say. She knew that Ronnie didn't mind hitting girls, because she'd seen him do it. So in the split second it took him to figure out just how angry he ought to be, she ducked under his arm and ran.

chapter

23

Dani ran, and a moment later she began to hear a clomping noise, as Ronnie came out of his trance and came after her. The heavy thud of boots was beginning to gain on her as she reached the entrance to the General Store and, on a sudden impulse, darted inside. It wasn't a well-thought-out move. The store, after all, was Grabler property and if anybody was there they'd probably be on Ronnie's side. But halfway down the aisle that separated hardware from groceries Dani suddenly knew where she was headed—behind the lunchroom counter, through the kitchen and out through the service door. The back door that opened directly onto the truck alley, and the path that led to the cabin. And then, unless a Grabler or one of their employees stopped her, she'd be safely home.

For once her luck held. No one the least bit dangerous was in the store. No one at all except for one plump, middle-aged clerk, way up on a ladder arranging things on a high shelf. Dani had time for a quick glimpse of a startled face way up above the grocery shelves as she dashed down the aisle, ducked under the lunch counter and darted into the kitchen. But it was there that her plan fell apart. The service door was locked.

Dani jerked frantically at the locked door as the sound of Ronnie's voice yelling questions at the clerk, and then the thud of his boots, got closer and louder. Definitely locked. She glanced around desperately, thinking, "Key? Key? No key. Another way out? Yes." She ran again then, across the kitchen to an alcove that opened into a short, dark hallway, and at its end some narrow wooden stairs that led up to another even darker hall. Dani had run up the stairs and was feeling her way, her eyes not yet adjusted to the lack of light, when suddenly something grabbed her from behind and jerked her backward, gasping and struggling, through a doorway.

"Shhh," a familiar voice was saying. "Be quiet." It was Stormy.

"Stormy," Dani said, "what on earth . . ."

"Shhh," he said again. "Listen."

She hushed then and listened. A series of thumps and thuds and clatters seemed to be coming from somewhere down below.

"Ronnie?" Stormy whispered, and Dani nodded.

"Yes," she whispered. "He was chasing me. But what's he doing? What's all that racket?"

"He's in the kitchen," Stormy said. "I think he's looking for you in the kitchen."

The thuds and clatters made sense then and Dani almost giggled, picturing Ronnie pawing through cupboards and closets.

But Stormy's voice still sounded worried. "He'll look here," he whispered. "He'll look here too."

He was probably right. Dani glanced around quickly. In the dim light of a tiny window she could barely make out a room the size of a large closet with nothing in it except a stack of wooden boxes and a narrow iron cot. Suddenly Stormy was pushing her toward the cot.

"Under the bed," he whispered urgently. "Hurry. He's coming."

It was stifling hot under the cot, the air thick with dust. Dani's heart was pounding so hard that it seemed to shake the floor. Fighting the possibility of a sneeze, and the even greater possibility of suffocation, she forced herself back against the wall, while above her head the metal springs of the cot squeaked rustily and then were still. Stormy had gotten back into the bed. There were footsteps on the stairs, then closer. The door banged open and a light blazed. Feet came into Dani's line of vision. Big feet in fancy cowboy boots.

"Hey, kid," Ronnie was saying, "did anyone come up here just now? Did you see anyone?"

The springs squeaked again and Stormy's voice said sleepily, "Nobody's here. Nobody's here 'cept me. I'm sick."

"Yeah?" Ronnie said. "You telling the truth?" The boots

came closer. "You better not be lying to me, kid." The springs creaked noisily.

"Turn me loose," Stormy said. "You're choking me. You better turn me loose."

"Oh yeah?" Ronnie laughed sarcastically. "I'd better, huh? Who's gonna make me?"

"Yeah." Stormy's voice had gone high and breathless. "You'd better. I might be catching. Like polio, maybe."

Ronnie laughed again, but the boots moved quickly back away from the bed and, a second later, went out the door. When the sound of footsteps on the stairs had died away, Stormy said, "Okay. You can come out now."

Pushing herself through clouds of choking dust, Dani crawled out and began to brush herself off. Stormy was sitting on the edge of the bed. He was wearing a huge baggy T-shirt instead of regular pajamas, and his feet and legs were bare. And now, in the brighter light, it was easy to see that he really did look sick. His whole face looked damp and pale, and there was a greenish tinge to his skin. Even his freckles seemed to have faded.

Dani stopped dusting and stared. "What is it?" she asked. "What's wrong with you? Do you really have . . ."

Stormy shook his head. "Not polio," he said. "Shrimp. Brenda's shrimp salad."

"Brenda fed you some bad shrimp salad?"

"Nope. She threw it out. But I found it."

"Food poisoning!" Dani was horrified. "You have food poisoning!"

175

Stormy's grin looked almost normal. "Not anymore," he said. "I threw it up."

"You're sure you're all right now?"

Stormy nodded confidently. "Now I am," he said.

Dani was really glad he was going to be all right, but the whole thing was getting to be slightly disgusting. Eating spoiled shrimp, and . . . She looked around. And the tiny, dusty room too. A bedroom that had probably been a storage closet for the old hotel. And only too obviously, the one thing it never had been was dusted. No wonder Stormy never wanted anyone to see where he lived.

"So this is your room?" Dani asked. "Yours—and your mother's?"

"No." Stormy looked offended. "My mother's room's down the hall." He pointed. "She got a big room." Suddenly he was looking uneasy. "You better go," he said.

"I will," Dani said. "But I have to tell you something first. Something very, very important."

Stormy nodded, looking serious and solemn. "Tell me," he said.

Lowering her voice, Dani said, "I'm leaving tomorrow. On the afternoon bus to Reno. I'm leaving tomorrow for Sea Grove."

Stormy stared at her for a long time without asking or arguing. He seemed to know she really meant it. After a long time he swallowed hard and said, "All right. Me too. I'm going too."

"Stormy," Dani said. "You can't. There isn't enough money. There's just barely enough for one person."

Stormy grabbed her arm. "But Pixie's going to get some more. For her birthday. She said so."

Dani sighed. "I know. She thinks she is. But her birthday isn't until next week. And she doesn't know when the money will come. I can't wait."

Stormy was still clutching her arm. "I'll come too," he said. "I'll get some money. You can't go without me. I won't . . ." He hushed then, saying, "Shhh. Listen."

Dani heard it then too. There were footsteps on the stairs again, but not the same kind of footsteps. Instead of a heavy thudding noise it was now a series of hard, sharp clicks. Sounds that might be made by someone in very high heels.

Pushing her back away from the door, Stormy put his finger to his lips and whispered, "Shhh. Stay here." Then he turned out the light and went out into the hall.

Standing there against the wall in the dimly lit room, Dani could hear voices, a woman's voice asking questions, and Stormy's answering. Hearing the voices, but not quite what they were saying, she suddenly felt frightened without knowing why. It was only Gloria out there, she was pretty sure of that. Only Stormy's mother, old Gorgeous Gloria.

What she should do, she told herself, was to open the door and walk out there and say, "Hi." Just say hello and tell Gloria the truth, that Ronnie had chased her and she'd run up there to get away from him. Anybody who knew Ronnie Grabler would understand that. That was what she ought to do, and she would have too, except for a mysterious feeling that tightened her throat, froze the muscles in her arms and legs and forced her to go on standing there in the dark, motionless and

177

silent. Made her stay right where she was in the tiny, stifling hot room until the voices stopped and, at last, Stormy came back into the room.

Closing the door behind him, Stormy held his finger to his lips and kept it there while the click of high heels was followed by the sound of another door opening and then closing. It wasn't until several minutes later, when the clicks had returned to pass Stormy's door again and continue down the stairs, that Stormy took his finger away from his lips. And it was then that, staring into his wide eyes, Dani began to understand where her own mysterious attack of fear had come from. She'd caught it from Stormy.

chapter

24

It wasn't until she was home again, back in the cabin with the front door locked and a chair pushed up against the broken lock on the back door, that Dani had time to start thinking. She thought first, of course, about Ronnie and whether he'd come looking for her at the cabin. She didn't think he would, but the locked door and the chair under the doorknob were just in case. With that taken care of there were many other things to consider, some of which she'd have preferred not to think about if she'd had the choice.

The part she really tried not to think about was what Ronnie had said about raising Linda's rent if she refused to sell her property, because that brought up a lot of other questions. Questions like what Linda would do if she had to pay more rent right now when she was about to lose her job at the bookstore. Dani tried her best to put the whole subject out of her mind by telling herself that what Linda would do was her business and nobody else's. She was the one who had chosen to stay in Rattler Springs and so how she was going to manage it was her own business. Dani had her own problems to think about. Problems like how she was going to manage the long, complicated bus trip to Sea Grove. Especially now that she knew for almost certain that no one would be going with her.

But her mind wouldn't cooperate. When she reminded herself of the big fight she and her mother had just had about selling the ranch to the Grablers, and how the whole thing had been Linda's fault from the very beginning for not doing enough to get them out of Rattler Springs long ago, her mind just kept coming back to the same questions. Questions about what would happen to Linda when she had no job and no place to live.

It was another unbearably hot day. Ordinarily Dani would have been out on the front porch by then, but because of the Ronnie problem, the best she could do was stay in the kitchen, where a wet towel draped over an open window could bring the temperature down a degree or two. By early afternoon what she was doing was trying to keep her mind on the right track by making a list of all the things she would need to take along on the trip. Which shirts and blouses, and maybe even a keepsake or two if they weren't too heavy. She hadn't gotten very far with the list when someone knocked on the front door.

Dani froze. Stormy, and Linda too, usually came in the back door. It might be Pixie, of course. Dani started to the living room. Or what if it was Ronnie? She stopped and went back to the kitchen, looking for something hard and heavy. When the knock came again she was headed for the door again, carrying a small cast-iron frying pan. Just as she got there she heard an impatient voice calling, "Dani! Let me in." It was Pixie after all.

When Dani unlocked the door Pixie kind of exploded into the room. She was wearing her khaki shorts and matching safari vest with lots of big stretchy pockets. As always, she was talking nonstop. "Dani," she said. "Where were you? Why didn't you let me in? My folks just have to make some phone calls in town and then they're going back, so I can't stay very long, but I have something to tell you. Something very important. What are you doing with that frying pan?"

"Oh, that." Dani looked down at what she had in her hand. "I guess I was getting ready to hit Ronnie Grabler over the head."

"Really?" Pixie looked delighted. "Could you? Could I help?" She stopped to catch her breath and added, "Why?"

"Because he chased me this morning. I made him mad so he chased me down the street and right through the store and under the lunch counter into the kitchen. I was going to run out through the service door only it was locked so I . . ." She paused. "I hid in . . . Well anyway I hid and got away from him. But I was afraid he might come here looking for me. When you knocked on the door I thought maybe he'd come."

"Really?" Pixie ran to the window and looked out. "I don't see him. Do you really think he'll come? I hope he comes

181

before my folks get back. Before . . ." Suddenly she put her hand over her mouth. "I forgot. I almost forgot what I came to tell you."

Reaching into one of the big pockets in her vest, she pulled out a fat envelope. "It came early," she said. "My birthday package from my grandmother. She always gives me a bunch of presents and a ten-dollar bill for every year, so there's eleven of them this time. Eleven ten-dollar bills. See. She usually gives it to me on my birthday but she mailed it early because she didn't know how long it would take to get here."

Staring at the fat roll of money, Dani opened her mouth to say—she didn't know what. After a moment she closed it again.

"Here." Pixie was holding out the money, pushing it toward her. "It's for the running-away fund." She shrugged. "If I was still at Grandma's I'd have to put most of it in the bank but here—well, nobody will notice what I do with it. It's not as much as the bicycle money would have been, but it's enough, isn't it?"

Holding Pixie's birthday money in her hands, Dani sat down on the edge of the daybed, and Pixie sat down beside her. Dani looked at the money, folding and unfolding it. It was more money than she'd ever before held in her own two hands.

"It's enough, isn't it?" Pixie was still asking. "Can we all go? All three of us?"

It was quite a while, maybe almost a minute before Dani said, "Yeah. It's enough."

"Then what's wrong?" Pixie asked. "Something's wrong, isn't it?"

Dani nodded. "Yes, something's wrong." She didn't know how to tell Pixie. In fact she didn't even know exactly what she was going to tell her until that moment when she admitted out loud that something was wrong with her decision to run away. She took a deep breath and, reaching over, she shoved the fat wad of money back into Pixie's lap. "What's wrong is," she said, "that I guess I can't go."

"You can't go?" Pixie's big eyes were electric with surprise. "But—But you said you had to. You said you were going to go no matter what."

"I know," Dani said. "I know." How could she explain? How could she explain in a way that someone like Pixie would understand? Someone who had never had to worry about whether there would be enough money to buy groceries at the end of the week or pay the next month's rent. There was no way she'd ever understand. And least of all would she ever understand about Linda. How could a kid who had parents who owned custom-built cars, not to mention a rich grandmother in San Francisco, understand about a mother who handled money problems by putting unpaid bills away out of sight and checking out another mushy novel?

"Dani?" Pixie was squirming impatiently. "Why don't you want to go anymore?"

"Look," Dani said. "It's not that I don't *want* to go. It's just that . . ." She stopped and started over. "Look. I'll tell you why I don't want to go if you tell me why you *do*. Okay?

Just the truth this time. Stormy isn't here so you don't have to drag in all that Frankenstein stuff. Just tell me why you really want to run away. Okay?"

Pixie stared at Dani and went on staring for a long time without moving or saying a word. For one of the longest times, in fact, that Dani had ever seen her sit with her mouth shut. And when she finally began to talk it was in a slow, uncertain voice, so that she hardly sounded like Pixie at all. "Why I want to run away?" she said slowly and thoughtfully. "Well, I guess it's just because I want to go back to my grandmother's." She looked at Dani and nodded and then went on sounding a little more like her normal self. "See, I thought I wanted to come out here and live with my parents but nobody else wanted me to. They all said I'd hate it. So I had to show them I meant it."

"How did you do that?" Dani asked.

Pixie's lips twitched and the fiery flicker was back in her eyes, at least for a second. "Oh, lots of ways," she said. "I stopped eating for one thing. And laughing. And talking too. I stopped talking to anyone."

Dani couldn't help smiling. "Wow. That must not have been easy."

"It wasn't," Pixie said. "But it worked. I think it was the not talking that did it. That really worried them."

"Yeah, I guess it would," Dani said. "So—you won and they let you come. And then you found out they'd been right, and you really did hate it?"

"Um, not really. I liked Rattler Springs and the school all right. I liked how different it all was. I thought school was kind of exciting. And you and Stormy. You and Stormy were the best part. But the part I hated was living with my parents. Living with my parents is absolutely the worst thing in the world."

Dani didn't get it. "Then why did you want to do it?" she asked. "You must have known what they were like."

Pixie shook her head. "No," she said. "I didn't. I guess I really didn't know. They've usually been off somewhere like Arabia or Brazil or Antarctica, at least since I was old enough to remember. They usually went someplace where kids weren't allowed. So I've been mostly with my grandmother. And I'd only see them at Grandma's house when they were home visiting for a little while. But then they came out here and it wasn't so far away, and it sounded all right to me, so . . ."

"Yeah, but what I still don't get," Dani said, "is what's so bad about them. I mean"—she grinned—"they're not really going to try to chop you up for monster parts or anything, and you don't get starved or—"

"Shhh. Listen." Pixie was cocking her head. "That's it. That's the car." On her knees on the daybed, she pushed back the drape. "Yes, there it . . ."

Dani looked too. It was the Smithsons' big black car, all right, coming up Silver Avenue. Coming up—passing the cabin—and going right on past.

Pixie jumped to her feet. On her way to the door she said, "See. They're forgetting about me. That's what's so awful. They're *always* forgetting about me."

She was gone then. Out into the middle of Silver Avenue, where she jumped up and down and waved her arms and yelled until the car came to a stop and slowly backed up. Backed up to where Pixie was waiting, with her hands on her hips.

When the huge black hulk of a car had disappeared up the avenue, Dani turned away from the window and collapsed. She lay there for a while thinking about what Pixie had told her, and also about what she'd told Pixie. And *why*. The *why* was what she thought about most.

It wasn't until she finally got up off the daybed that she noticed a big fat wad of ten-dollar bills lying on the floor not far from where Pixie had been sitting.

chapter

25

It was some time later that Dani realized how long she'd been standing there. Just standing there in the middle of the room, staring at all that money. She glanced at the clock. Linda might show up at any minute. Dani hurried to her room then and, after counting the eleven bills once more, she tucked them away next to the running-away-fund envelope at the back of her underwear drawer. She would give it back to Pixie the next time she came, all one hundred and ten dollars of it, but in the meantime it needed to be where it wouldn't be noticed and have to be explained.

Back in the kitchen she just had time to throw away the packing list she'd been working on and pull the chair out from under the doorknob when Linda came up the back steps.

Dinner at the O'Donnells that night was polite enough, but

not exactly relaxed. It probably had something to do with the fact that both Dani and her mother were working so hard at not talking about certain subjects.

The subject that Dani's head was full of, but that she absolutely couldn't bring up, was her decision not to run away. You couldn't just come out and tell your mother that you'd decided not to run away after all, especially when she'd never known that you were planning to in the first place. And you certainly couldn't tell her why you weren't. At least not until you'd finished figuring it out for yourself.

And as for Linda, she was probably trying not to mention the terrible fight they'd had the night before and all the mean things they'd said to each other. And both of them were trying to not even mention the Grablers' offer and what Linda was going to do about it. So they couldn't talk about the quarrel, or about the ranch, or the Grablers. Or even about the bookstore, because of the fact that Linda was about to lose her job there. It was as if they'd made this silent agreement that they weren't going to mention anything that might start another fight. But the trouble was, that didn't seem to leave very many topics. Dani didn't know what on earth they would have had to talk about if it hadn't been for Stormy.

The subject of Stormy came up as soon as they sat down to eat. Linda suddenly looked around and said, "Still no sign of Stormy? Was he here at all today?"

"No," Dani said, "but I found out why he hasn't been here. He's been sick."

"Sick?" Linda looked worried.

"Oh, he's better now," Dani said quickly. "He said it was something he ate."

"I'm not surprised," Linda said. "He seems to live on the most awful trash. I don't think his mother ever cooks for him." She sighed. "But then maybe there's no way she could. I don't suppose they even have a kitchen of their own."

"No, they don't. They just have two hotel rooms. Stormy's is about as big as a closet."

Linda looked at her curiously. "Have you seen their rooms? I thought you said he didn't ever let anyone see where he lives."

"That's right," Dani said quickly. "He never did want me to see it." She considered mentioning how she'd happened to wind up there and the whole thing about the Ronnie problem. But that would involve telling what she'd said to Ronnie that made him so mad. In the end she decided to say simply, "I never did see it until this morning. That was how I found out about him being sick."

Linda smiled. "It was good of you to visit him, Dani," she said. "I should at least have asked Gloria about him, but I didn't want to go looking for her and risk running into the Grablers until . . ." She stopped and got up quickly to light the burner under the teakettle. When she came back to the table she asked, "But you're sure he is getting better?"

"Yeah," Dani said. "I guess he ate some shrimp salad that the Grablers threw out, and it gave him food poisoning."

"Oh dear." Linda looked shocked.

"I know," Dani said. "But he said he felt better after he

threw it up. He'll probably be here for breakfast. I'll bet he'll be here first thing in the morning."

That was all she said out loud but as she headed for her room she was thinking that Stormy would have lots of reasons to show up bright and early tomorrow. There was, for instance, the fact that tomorrow would be Thursday, and the last thing Stormy had heard was that Thursday would be Dani's last day in Rattler Springs. So he'd be right there, for sure, trying to talk her into waiting until he could come too. She smiled a little, picturing Stormy's amazement when he found out she wasn't going to leave after all. But then he certainly would ask why. She stopped smiling then, and for the next hour or so, while she got ready for bed and waited to go to sleep, she tried to decide exactly how she was going to answer that question. Waking up the next morning, she still wasn't sure. She'd start, she told herself, by simply saying she'd changed her mind, and then just wait and see what came out of her mouth next.

But Stormy wasn't there for breakfast. Linda made lots of oatmeal and waited until she was almost late for work. At the door she stopped long enough to say, "I'm worried about him, Dani. I'll ask about him when I'm at the hotel." She paused, looked at Dani quickly and then looked away before she said, "You know I have to give the Grablers my answer sometime today?"

"Yeah. I know," Dani said shrugging. "And you're going to say no." Linda was watching her closely and if Dani didn't let her face say that she understood, it was because she still didn't. Not exactly anyway. But when the door closed and the sound of footsteps on the stairs died away, she suddenly got up and went to the window. Pushing aside the curtain, she looked out and watched while her mother picked her way along the narrow path between puncture vines and hedgehog cactus on her way to the alley. Watched her picking her way carefully through the thorns in her sandals and then, when she reached the alley, lifting her head and squaring her shoulders before she walked on down the alley toward the bookstore and the meeting with the Grabby Grablers. And it was right then that Dani really began to understand not only why Linda had to stand up to the Grablers, but also why she herself had to stay in Rattler Springs and help her do it.

It was only a minute or two later and Dani was still standing at the window when she became aware of some familiar thumps and clatters that seemed to be coming from the direction of Silver Avenue. It didn't seem likely, so early in the morning, but it sounded suspiciously like the arrival of Pixie and the Black Phantom. Thinking, "She's come for her money," Dani headed for the front of the house.

"Hi," a red-faced, sweaty Pixie said as Dani opened the door. "I came early so it wouldn't be so hot. My mother will pick me up around eleven. Is that all right? I wanted to talk to you. Is Stormy here? Wheee ooh! I'm hot. May I have some water?"

She headed for the kitchen and Dani followed her. It wasn't until Pixie was busy drinking that Dani managed to say, "I guess you came for the money. I found it on the floor after—"

"The money? Oh yes," Pixie said. "I wondered what happened to it. Did I leave it here?" Putting down the glass, she

191

held her hands under the faucet and splashed water on her face and arms. "Oooh, that feels good." Still splashing, she began to ask about Stormy. "Have you told Stormy yet? Have you told him you're not going to run away? What did he say? Did you tell him I got enough birthday money to pay for the tickets, but you still won't run away?"

Dani waited. When Pixie finally ran down she said, "Look, Pixie. If you'd hush up for a minute I'd tell you." She talked fast then, trying to get in what needed to be said before Pixie got going again. "About Stormy—he still hasn't been here, but I know why now. I forgot to tell you yesterday. He's been sick. He doesn't know yet that I've changed my mind about running away. He thinks I'm leaving today."

"Sick?" Pixie looked shocked and sorry, but at the same time kind of excited. "Is it serious, like polio or scarlet fever? They thought I had scarlet fever once but it was only measles. I wanted it to be scarlet fever because they were going to quarantine us. My mother and father too, and they weren't going to let them go to Patagonia. But it was only measles, and they went." She stopped for breath and then asked again, "What does Stormy have?"

When Dani explained about Stormy and the spoiled shrimp, Pixie shivered and said, "Ugh. That's awful."

"I know," Dani said. "But he's probably all right by now." She was just starting to tell about seeing Stormy in his room and how he'd said he was getting better when she became aware of the sound of footsteps. Footsteps slowly crossing the kitchen, the squeak of a hinge—and then there he was. Stormy himself.

Dani jumped to her feet. "Stormy," she said. "Where have you been? Are you still sick?"

' "No. Not sick." He shook his head in a funny crooked way, holding it a little to one side, and his voice was whispery.

He sounded, Dani thought, as if he was trying to speak without moving his lips. But it wasn't until she'd started across the room toward him that she began to see and understand. Began to see that something was terribly wrong with Stormy's face. His right eye was almost swollen shut and there was a big dark bruise all around it, and both his lips were swollen and caked with blood. As she approached he backed away, holding her off with both hands.

"Don't," he whispered. "It hurts."

"Stormy." Dani's voice was sharp with anger. "Who beat you up? Was it Ronnie? It was Ronnie, wasn't it?"

He shook his head again in that strange, careful way. "No. Not Ronnie," he said. "It was . . ." He looked away, refusing to meet Dani's eyes. "It wasn't her fault. I stole her tip money. She was awful mad."

Dani gasped. Pixie was beside her then, whispering and jabbing her shoulder, trying to get her attention. "Who?" Pixie whispered. "Who did it?"

Lowering her voice, Dani breathed the answer into Pixie's ear. "His mother. His mother beat him up."

chapter
26

His face wasn't the worst of it. Later in the kitchen while Stormy was trying to eat watered-down oatmeal without moving his lips, Pixie pulled Dani around behind him and pointed to where, below his shorts, you could see big purple welts up and down the backs of his legs. Pointing to the welts, Pixie had begun to ask, "Stormy, what—?" when Dani shushed her and pulled her away. It wasn't until Pixie agreed to keep her mouth shut by putting her own finger to her lips and nodding in agreement that Dani allowed her to come back and sit down at the table.

Sitting there across the table while Stormy ate, watching how slowly and painfully the oatmeal was disappearing, and comparing it to the way he usually disposed of food, Dani felt her throat tightening with fury. Like Pixie, she desperately wanted to ask about what had happened and why. But that sort of question, she kept telling herself, would have to wait. When the oatmeal was finally gone, Stormy began to talk without being questioned. He started, however, by asking some questions of his own.

His first question was, "You going today, Dani? You running away today?"

It wasn't until that moment that it suddenly dawned on Dani how much of what had happened had been, at least partly, her own fault. It wasn't hard to guess why he had tried to steal Gloria's tip money. Not when she, Dani, had just told him that she was going to run away today, and that he wouldn't be able to come with her because *there wasn't enough money to pay for his tickets.*

Suddenly Dani could see what must have happened almost as clearly as if she'd been there. She could see how, after he'd talked to her, he'd been so desperate to get ticket money that he'd gone into Gloria's room to look for some—and how Gloria must have caught him taking her money. And maybe she'd had a lot to drink at the time. Dani had heard, everyone in town had heard, about how Gloria acted sometimes when she'd had too much to drink.

"Are you going?" Stormy was repeating. "Today?"

"No! No!" Dani almost shouted. "I'm not going. I've decided not to go at all. Or at least not for a long time."

Stormy stared at her wide-eyed, and then started his wide jack-o'-lantern grin. Started, winced with pain, and stopped. But his voice had a grin in it as he said, "*Okay.* That's okay then."

"Stormy," Dani found herself asking, "when did she . . . ?"

He frowned and shook his head.

Dani's nod told him she understood what mustn't be talked about. "When did you get hurt?"

His eyes fell. "Last night. It was last night." But then he looked up quickly. "She was sorry this morning. Really sorry. She brought me a real breakfast. From the cafe. Ham and eggs." For a moment his eyes, even the swollen one, had that familiar hungry gleam, but then it faded. "Only I couldn't eat it. Too much chewing." He thought for a moment. "She told me not to come here today. She said I had to stay home. But I didn't because I thought you were . . ."

Dani nodded. "Because you thought I was leaving."

"Umm," he agreed. He started to stand up then, so slowly and painfully that Dani jumped up to help, but he held her off. "No, don't," he said. At the door he stopped, looked at Pixie, and asked, "Did you ride here? On the Black Phantom?"

Pixie nodded. "Yes," she said. "It's on the front porch."

For a moment Stormy looked longingly toward the front door. Then he shook his head slightly and said, "I'm going to the bathroom. Okay?"

When he disappeared Dani and Pixie went on sitting at the table, and for several minutes neither of them had anything to say. Now and then they looked at each other. Pixie's eyes were bleak, blue marbles. Huge and round as always, but without the usual fireworks.

Stormy was gone such a long time that, after a while, Dani

went to see if he was all right. When she came back she told Pixie that she had found him in her bedroom. "He's asleep," she said. "Sound asleep. He probably didn't sleep much last night."

Pixie nodded and asked the same question that Dani had been asking herself. "What are we going to do?"

Dani shook her head, and went on shaking it, fighting against a frightening feeling of helplessness. "I don't know," she said.

"Could you just keep him here?" Pixie asked.

"I don't think it would work. Gloria would just come and get him. She did once before when my mom let him stay a long time."

She was still thinking about Gloria, thinking about the time she'd screamed at Linda for letting Stormy stay over, when suddenly there was a loud knocking noise. Not on the door but on the kitchen window. Talk about coincidence. Somehow, even before she looked up and saw her peering in at them, Dani knew who it would be.

Pixie was staring too. But as Dani got to her feet Pixie tugged at her arm. There was a halfway smile on her lips and a small electric flicker was back in her eyes. "Dani," she whispered. "We haven't seen him, have we? We're worried about him. But we *haven't* seen him."

Dani nodded and went to the door.

"Hi, Gloria," she said. "Did you want to see my mother? She's still at the bookstore."

Gloria was wearing a sharp-looking purple skirt and a lavender sweater. Except for some smeared eye makeup and the wild tangle of her blond hair, she seemed about the same as always. Her smile looked unreal, but no more than usual. "Hi there, girls," she said, trying to see past them into the kitchen. "Has my kid been here this morning?"

"You're looking for Stormy?" Dani asked.

"Yeah," Gloria said. "I need to find him. I—He had a little accident last night. Fell down some stairs. You know, those steep stairs over at the hotel. Banged himself up some. I need to see if he's all right."

"Oh," Dani said. "Well, if we see him we'll—"

But then Pixie took over, pushing Dani aside and stepping in front of her. Her eyes had that familiar flicker as she said, "An accident? Oh dear. How terrible. Did he break any bones?" Gloria seemed to be trying to answer, but Pixie didn't wait for it. "We haven't seen him for a long time, have we, Dani? We've really been wondering where he's been lately. Would you like us to help you hunt for him? We could do that. Couldn't we, Dani?"

But Gloria was shaking her head and backing away, trying to keep her balance as her high-heeled shoes sank into the sandy path. "No, no. Real sweet of you kids to offer, but not necessary. I'm sure he'll turn up soon."

They watched her go, until she had disappeared down the alley and around the corner of the hotel, before Dani went in to check on Stormy. He was still sound asleep.

Back in the kitchen the two of them sat at the table again for a long time without speaking. For Pixie, an amazingly long time. But when they started to talk it was both at once. Not using the same words exactly but what they said meant the same thing. What Dani said was, "I guess I'll have to run away after all, and take Stormy with me."

And what Pixie said was, "Yes. And I'll go too."

There was another long pause before Pixie said, "When?"

"Today, I guess," Dani said. "Like I was planning. After today it would be too late. She'd find him and take him back."

Pixie nodded and went on nodding. After a while she said, "How?"

"That's what we have to figure out," Dani said. "Plans. We have to make plans."

"Okay," Pixie said. "We'll make . . ." She hushed then, cocking her head and listening. "It's the car," she said. "My mother's coming." She got slowly to her feet.

"What are you going to do?" Dani asked.

"Shhh." Pixie's voice was firm. "I'm planning." She disappeared into the living room and then Dani heard her footsteps on the front porch. In a minute or two she came back. "I asked her if I could stay longer, and I can. I said we were right in the middle of working a puzzle and we just have to finish it. Which is kind of the truth, huh?" Her small white teeth flashed in an innocent smile. "It's nice when things can be kind of the truth. Isn't it? So—anyway she said all right. She said they have to meet someone in town later tonight so I can stay till then."

"We'll be gone by then," Dani said.

Pixie smiled again, but this time it didn't look so innocent. "I know," she said. "Let's plan."

The first part of the plan was buying the tickets, which,

because of Pixie's birthday money, shouldn't be a problem. At least not a financial one.

"But we'll have to be careful about Mrs. Arlen," Dani told Pixie.

"Mrs. Arlen? Who's she?"

"She runs the post office, and sells bus tickets too," Dani told her. "But she's real nosey. Like if I went in there and bought three tickets, one adult and two for kids, she'd want to know if the adult was my mother and if I was going to try to pretend I wasn't twelve yet. And if she found out who the tickets were really for, it would be all over town in five minutes."

"So," Pixie said, "what are you going to tell her?"

Dani shook her head. "I don't know. I'll think about it."

"Hmm." Pixie squinted. "I know what I could tell her. So I'll buy the tickets. Okay?"

Dani said she guessed that would be okay, and then she made the mistake of asking Pixie what she was planning to tell Mrs. Arlen.

"Well." Pixie thought for only a split second before she said, "I'd tell her the tickets are for my aunt Cassandra and my cousins who came to see us a few days ago." She paused but only for a second or two and then went on. "See, they came in their car, which is this big long Oldsmobile convertible—a green Oldsmobile convertible—only it broke down—and they can't wait until it's fixed so they're going to take the bus to Reno and then home to San Francisco—they have to get home right away because my oldest cousin—Edwina—my oldest cousin's name is Edwina—she just had her eleventh birthday so she's not too old for a child's ticket—well, Edwina has to play her violin in a concert on Saturday, so they just have to be home on time—see, my cousin Edwina is a famous violinist and she—"

"Pixie," Dani interrupted. "Is your cousin really a famous violinist?"

Pixie shook her head. "I don't know," she said, grinning. "I don't think I have a cousin named Edwina."

It was about then that Dani decided that Pixie really should be the one to buy the tickets. After all, most of the money was hers. And besides, if Nosey Rosie started asking questions this time, she'd get more answers than she'd know what to do with.

So with that decided, Dani went back to working on other parts of the plan. The hardest part, she decided, the almost impossibly hard part, when you really thought about it, would be getting Stormy down to the bus stop and onto the bus. To get him across town and up Main Street without Gloria spotting him, or anyone who might know by then that he was missing. She'd had a couple of ideas, but nothing that seemed very possible, when Pixie asked what else needed to be worked on.

When Dani explained the problem, Pixie's first suggestion was that they should have Stormy wear a disguise. "Maybe we could dress him up like a girl with a wig with lots of curly hair that would kind of hang down and hide . . ."

Pixie was still gesturing with both hands to show how the curls would cover most of Stormy's face, when she suddenly froze and said, "Oh, hi, Stormy. You woke up. Hey, guess what? Dani changed her mind again. We're going to run away after all."

"Yeah, I heard," Stormy said. As he shuffled toward them Dani was able to recognize, even through all the cuts and bruises, a typical Stormy frown. The kind that usually meant there was no use arguing with him. And in a strange way, it was good to see him being his normally stubborn self. "No dress," he said. "I won't wear a dress."

"That's all right," she told him quickly. "You won't have to. For one thing, we don't have a wig. We'll think of some other way, won't we, Pixie?"

So Stormy sat down with them at the table and they went on working on how to get him to the bus stop at five o'clock that afternoon without anyone seeing him.

Pixie's next suggestion was that they find a wheelbarrow big enough for Stormy to curl up in, cover him with a blanket and push him down Main Street to the bus stop.

"No, I don't think so," Dani said. She might have pointed out that curling up in a wheelbarrow wouldn't be too comfortable for a person who'd just been beaten half to death, but she settled for saying that she didn't know anyone who had a wheelbarrow big enough to hold a nine-year-old kid.

The plan they finally settled on was mostly Stormy's idea. "We could go out to the gully," he said pointing away from town, toward the east, "and down the flash flood tunnel. And then way out around to Gus's. To the back of Gus's."

Dani understood immediately. She explained it to Pixie by saying they would head out away from town in the wrong direction until they came to a dry gully that led to the tunnel that went under the highway about a half mile north of town. And from there they could circle back to where Gus's property started, without going through any places where they were likely to be seen.

Pixie said she thought her own ideas were a lot more exciting, and that Stormy's suggestion sounded kind of boring and uncomfortable. Uncomfortable, as in walking all that way on such a hot day.

Dani had to agree with her. "Yeah," she said, "hot and boring. But what's good about it is that it doesn't depend on stuff we don't have, like wigs or wheelbarrows. And the other good thing is—it just might work."

Pixie still wasn't convinced. "But there's nothing to hide behind out there on the desert," she said.

Dani nodded. "I know. Except when you're in the gully. Then you're out of sight for a while. And once we get to Gus's property there's plenty of stuff to hide behind. There's enough junk on Gus's property to hide an army. And besides, there will just be the two of us. Stormy and me. You can go downtown and buy the tickets. And meet us at the bus stop. You know where the bus stops, don't you? Right there in Gus's parking lot? And by yourself you'll be all right. Nobody will be looking for you. Not till after the bus has left anyway."

So it was all decided and there was nothing left to do but try to eat a little lunch, get the money out of Dani's underwear drawer and pack the duffel bag. The lunch wasn't too successful. Dani made peanut butter sandwiches but both she and Pixie were too excited to eat, and it hurt Stormy too much to open his mouth.

Packing the duffel bag turned out to be quite different from Dani's original plan. Because neither Stormy nor Pixie had spare clothing, or any chance to get any, Dani decided she wouldn't take any either. Instead she filled the bag with things like sun lotion, Mercurochrome and bandages, two Thermos bottles of water and the leftover peanut butter sandwiches.

So that was it. Dani O'Donnell was finally about to do what she'd been planning to do for so long. "All right," she said. "Let's get started." But as the others were going out the back door she suddenly turned and went back.

"Wait. Wait a minute," she called. "I forgot something important."

In her bedroom, she got out her notebook and ripped out a sheet of paper. Writing fast, scribbling almost, she wrote:

Dear Mother,

I'm running away with Stormy and Pixie. Pixie has enough money for tickets all the way to Sea Grove. I'm going because Stormy has to get away from Gloria. I'd decided not to go until I saw how she'd almost killed him.

Dani

Reading it over quickly, she knew she'd done a poor job, but she thought Linda might understand. In fact, she was pretty sure her mother would understand. She smoothed out the paper and added one more word, just before her name. The word was *love*.

LOVE, Dani

She left the note in her underwear drawer where it surely would be found eventually. Eventually, but not before the Thursday bus was well on its way.

They started out then. Pixie and the money left first, heading toward town. And then it was Dani and Stormy's turn. At the door Stormy stopped and looked back, toward the front of the house, and said, "The Black Phantom?"

Dani shook her head firmly. "No, we can't," she said. "We can't take a bicycle."

Stormy nodded sadly. "No," he said. "I guess not."

chapter

27

It was midafternoon when Dani and Stormy started out across the open desert. The sun was still high in the sky, and fiercely hot. Its rays beat straight down on Dani's head and its fiery breath scorched her lungs. But it wasn't just the desert's boring old threats that were making her heart beat faster. Not this time. Right at first it was simply the fear of being seen by someone Gloria had sent out to look for Stormy. Or perhaps by kids who'd recognize them and who, a few minutes later, would blab about them all over town. Or by nosey adults who would ask what they were doing, and what on earth had happened to Stormy's face.

Time passed, twenty blazing, sweating minutes, or maybe more, before there weren't any yards or houses close enough to be a threat. But that didn't mean they were home safe. Who knew when they might meet up with a bunch of kids out snake hunting or exploring? Or when someone, driving up Silver Avenue, might happen to look out across the desert toward the north?

It was easy to see that Stormy was trying to walk as fast as he could, but even so Dani had to stop and wait every few minutes, clenching her teeth to keep from telling him to hurry. And once, when a truck roared by on Silver Avenue, she dropped to the ground and yelled, "Stormy. Get down," before she stopped to think. He got down all right, but when the danger was past, it wasn't easy to get him back up. The pain on his face as he struggled to his feet made Dani's throat swell and throb. With anger mostly, but also with a strange urge to yell and scream, or maybe to cry.

Farther away from town she was able to relax a little and concentrate on keeping Stormy moving slowly and steadily toward the dry gully. The gully, or Horny Toad Gulch as it was sometimes called, wasn't much bigger than a deep ditch. According to rumor, it had been formed by water running down from the hills during flash floods. But there hadn't been a flood in many years and, as far as Dani knew, the gully bed was always dry and empty. Empty, that is, except for a tumble of jagged boulders, and now and then a sudden speedy slither, when you crossed the path of some awful desert creature. Dani knew kids who thought the gully was an exciting playground, but to her it had always been an evil place. The kind of place where the desert's voices had always been especially loud and clear.

And the gully was also—*hot*. Shut off from even the slightest trace of breeze, the deep ditch seemed to concentrate the heat, bouncing it back and forth off its rocky walls. As they followed its bed with maddening slowness, waves of heat beat against their faces, and lizards, or something worse, skittered away at their approach. They had almost reached the place where the gully ran under the highway when Dani noticed that Stormy was staggering.

She went back to walk beside him as his shuffling steps slowed, then stopped. As Dani grabbed his arm he lurched and almost fell. Holding him up, she looked around frantically. There was no escape from the sun anywhere, except up ahead where the western wall of the gully deepened to meet the tunnel under the highway. "Come on, Stormy," she whispered in his ear. "Just a few more steps and we'll rest. There, in the shade."

He nodded and stumbled on, to where he could lean against the wall while Dani cleared away some rocks and helped him to sit. They stayed there for a long time. Stormy seemed totally exhausted, almost unconscious. His face was wet with sweat and his tanned and freckled skin looked strangely colorless, except for the dark smudge of bruises around his eyes and mouth. Dani wondered if he would ever be able to get up and go on.

The water in the Thermos was lukewarm but at least it was wet and when she held the cup up to Stormy's swollen lips he swallowed eagerly. And then, when he stopped swallowing, she drank a little herself before she dribbled the rest slowly over Stormy's head and face. A few minutes later his eyes flicked open and he said, "That felt good."

His eyes closed again, but it seemed to Dani that he was breathing more normally. She waited through many more sweltering minutes before he opened his eyes and looked around. Up the gully first and then down toward the tunnel and back to focus on Dani. He stared at her, and then his eyes rolled up toward the sky. "What's it saying?" he whispered.

"What's what saying?" Dani asked.

Stormy glanced upward, frowning. "The desert?" he said.

She understood then and, following Stormy's gaze, she looked up at the desert sky for a long moment before she whispered, "Hey. I don't know. I've been too busy to listen."

He nodded and closed his eyes and when they opened again he began to struggle to his feet. "Come on," he said. "We'll miss the bus."

Dani had thought about that. The narrow slice of shade had widened noticeably since they'd first sat down. She looked up at the sky, where the sun was now much closer to the western horizon. It must be at least five by now or even later, and there was still a long way to go. Missing the bus was a real possibility. "Right," she said. "Let's get going."

The tunnel under the highway came next. It was actually only a large drainage pipe, but large enough for a kid Stormy's size to walk through standing almost erect. Dani had been dreading it. In fact she'd been forcing herself not to think about it until she had to. Rumor had it that anyone who wanted to catch a rattlesnake had only to go to the tunnel on a hot day and the snakes would be there, escaping the midday sun. At the tunnel mouth she stopped.

"Snakes?" Stormy asked, and Dani nodded.

"I hate snakes," she said. "Especially rattlers."

"Yeah," Stormy said, "I know." After a while he said, "We could throw rocks."

"Rocks?" Dani was asking, but then she got the picture. If they threw enough rocks into the tunnel to drive the snakes out the other side, they might be able to make it through without meeting one. It was worth a try. So she gathered up rocks and began to throw. She'd never been much good at throwing, either baseballs or rocks, and the things she did throw didn't always go where she wanted them to. After a while Stormy began to help, not bending to pick up rocks but throwing the ones Dani handed him, not hard but accurately. Once or twice after a rock landed, Dani was sure she heard an ominous rattling sound. They'd thrown a lot of rocks before they started through.

The light was dim in the tunnel and it got dimmer as they moved forward. At least Stormy moved forward. Dani's feet seemed out of control, refusing to budge, while her ears worked overtime, listening frantically for any sound that might be the beginning of a rattle or slither. By the time they'd reached the other side Stormy was definitely leading the way. His voice seemed stronger too, although he was still talking through almost motionless lips. "I guess the rocks chased them out," he said. "Or else it was time for them to go hunting." He looked up at the sky. "See," he said. "It's getting late."

He was right and, with the tunnel out of the way, Dani could concentrate on their next big problem. The time. One advantage of not being able to afford a wristwatch was that you developed a feeling for the time of day. And at the moment it felt late, like maybe six o'clock or even later. If the bus happened to be on time for once, it might already have come and gone. But there was nothing to do but push on and hope that it would be late, as usual.

The rest of their route led westward through the gully until they were well past the Sagebrush Motor Lodge and the outskirts of Rattler Springs. It was then that they climbed out of the ditch and headed back toward town. They had to pass through Old Town first, where what used to be a residential area was now a shamble of tumbledown buildings that hadn't been occupied since the silver mine closed. Just beyond the last crumbling, roofless cabin they came to the straggle of broken fencing that marked the western edge of Gus's property. And the beginning of Gus's junkyard.

Dani had always despised junkyards as the ugliest and most depressing places on earth, but now she found herself appreciating all the huge, rusty carcasses of long-dead cars and trucks, and even wishing there were a few more of them. A few more enormous hulks for her and Stormy to shelter behind as they moved slowly toward town and the bus stop. The sun was low now in the west and the air seemed a little cooler, but Dani was beginning to feel exhausted, and terribly hungry. She knew it must be very late, certainly way past dinnertime. And Stormy was wobbling again.

As Dani turned to watch him he stopped to lean carefully against an old station wagon, and again, a minute later, on the radiator of a truck. "What is it?" Dani asked him. "Are you all right?"

"I—don't—know," he whispered. "I feel funny."

He staggered then and Dani grabbed him as he sank to the ground. Propping him up against the truck's front wheel, she opened the duffel bag and got out the last Thermos. It wasn't until she had poured water over his head and face and managed to dribble a little between his lips that his eyes opened. "What happened?" he asked. "Was I asleep?"

"I think you fainted," Dani said. "Did you? Do you think you fainted?"

"I don't know," Stormy said. "Maybe." His eyes, even the poor swollen one, rolled thoughtfully before he said, "I think I'm hungry."

Dani grinned and said, "I know. So am I." And Stormy must be famished. There had been the food poisoning and then, before he'd fully recovered, the swollen lips problem. Pawing through the stuff in the duffel bag, she said ruefully, "All I have is some squashed peanut butter sandwiches."

Stormy nodded stiffly and said, "Squashed is okay."

A few minutes later Dani left Stormy propped up against the wheel of a truck, eating peanut butter sandwiches by pulling off tiny pieces and pushing them carefully between his swollen lips. Dani hurried off to look for Pixie. For Pixie— and the Thursday bus to Reno.

She had almost reached the garage where Gus repaired cars, and dangled people he didn't like over his grease pit, when, out of nowhere, an angry voice called her name. Dani jumped, stumbled and almost fell as she looked frantically in every direction.

"Where have you been? You're late," the voice went on.

212

And then there she was. Pixie Smithson was sitting on the backseat of a wheel-less, windowless sedan. Sitting there comfortably, looking cool and collected in her stylish safari shorts —and eating a huge hamburger sandwich.

"Pixie," Dani said. "I know we're late. But we couldn't hurry. Stormy's been too sick. Has the bus gone? Have we missed the bus?"

"Here. Hold this." Handing Dani the hamburger, Pixie started to crawl out through a window. "No, we haven't missed it," she said as she came out legs first and slithered down to the ground. "The bus is late. I bought the tickets and I've been going back to the post office every few minutes to ask about it. At least I was until Mrs. Arlen went home. Mrs. Arlen said the bus's radiator must be boiling again. Anyway, it hasn't come yet." She looked at her wristwatch. "Every ten minutes I go out to the parking lot to see—" She shrugged. "But so far, no bus."

Dani was relieved to hear that they hadn't missed the bus after all, but with that worry taken care of the look and smell of the big, juicy hamburger took over. She only halfway heard the rest of what Pixie was saying. Something about all the things she'd been doing while she waited. One of which had obviously been done at the Silver Grill. Dani swallowed hard and, without even deciding to, took a big bite of hamburger sandwich.

"Hey," Pixie said. "You're eating my sandwich."

"I know," Dani said with her mouth full. "I couldn't help it. Come on. I'm taking the rest of it to Stormy. We're starving."

They found Stormy right where Dani had left him, propped up against the wheel of the truck, but to her relief, the shade and the peanut butter seemed to have helped. He was looking and sounding a lot more normal. And when he saw the half-eaten hamburger he looked even more like his old self. Clutching what was left of the sandwich in both hands, he managed a one-sided grin before he began to eat by using his peanut butter sandwich technique, breaking off little pieces and squashing them before he pushed them between his lips. He was getting better at it, but it was still a slow process. Before the hamburger was gone Pixie and Dani had each taken a turn sneaking out to the parking lot to check on the bus. When Pixie came back for the second time she was running. "Come on," she called as she skidded to a stop. "It's here. The bus came. Hurry."

chapter
28

They hurried toward the bus stop, or at least went as fast as Stormy could shuffle. But, as it turned out, they needn't have. When they reached the parking lot the bus was there all right, but the passengers were all on their way across the street heading for the Silver Grill or the bar at the Grand Hotel. They watched from behind a beat-up old Buick as the bus driver, a tall, scrawny man wearing a sweat-stained uniform, locked the bus door and followed his passengers across the street and into the restaurant.

"There he goes," Dani said angrily, slamming her fist down on the fender of the car. "He's already two or three hours late and now he's going off to have dinner. We're not going to get out of here for hours, and by then everyone in town will be looking for us."

"I know," Pixie said, and then she added, "I'll find out how long it will be." Before Dani could stop her she took off running across the lot and the road, and disappeared into the Silver Grill.

"Well, that's it," Dani said to Stormy. "She's going to get us caught for sure."

Stormy swallowed the last of the hamburger before he asked, "Do they know about us?"

"Does who know?"

"The cafe people?"

Dani shrugged. "No. I don't suppose so. But the Smithsons might be looking for Pixie by now. And my mother too. My mother might go in there looking for me. She's probably been home by now and . . ."

She stopped as she was suddenly seeing, almost as if it were happening on a kind of movie screen inside her head, her mother walking in the door and calling out the way she always did. Calling out and then beginning to look around the cabin. Imagining Linda searching more and more frantically, caused a sharp pain in Dani's chest and a swollen feeling in her throat. She swallowed hard, telling herself she was being ridiculous. After all, it was a little late to start worrying about how Linda would take it when she found out that her only kid had disappeared. Dani was still telling herself she was being ridiculous, and to just stop thinking about it, when Pixie dashed back across the lot.

"Hi," she said excitedly. "I found out everything. I talked to the bus driver and he said they'd be leaving soon. I told

216

him we'd been waiting for hours and there were three of us. And he said there was plenty of room and that he'd be leaving in half an hour. So we're all set. We just have to keep hidden until the bus leaves."

They went on waiting, watching from behind the old Buick while the short desert twilight deepened toward night and Rattler Springs Main Street became dim and shadowy. But then, finally, things began to happen.

The first thing Dani noticed was a familiar figure coming down the street and crossing over to the parking lot. A huge mountain of a man with a dome-shaped head surrounded by straggly hair. It had to be Gus. And then, about the time Gus reached his parking lot, the bus driver emerged from the Silver Grill and came back across the street. Peering carefully around the Buick, Dani and Pixie watched while Gus and the bus driver chatted and worked on the bus, filling the gas tank and doing things under the hood.

"Get ready," Dani whispered. "Pixie, where are the tickets?" When Pixie had given them each a ticket, a blue adult one for Dani and green ones for herself and Stormy, Dani said, "Now. As soon as Gus goes back inside the station we'll start out. We should just walk calmly over to the bus, give the driver our tickets and get on."

Pixie nodded excitedly. "Yes," she said. "We'll walk right over and get on."

"Calmly," Stormy said. "After Gus goes away."

Only it didn't turn out to be that easy.

The bus driver said no. The scrawny, sweaty bus driver

looked at the three of them and at their tickets, and then he shook his head and said, "No way, kids. 'Fraid I can't let you on without a parent's say-so."

"But I told you," Pixie almost shrieked. "I told you about how our mother was dying and we don't have any father so we were going to go live with our aunt in Reno. I told you in the restaurant, and you said okay."

"Yep, you told me that," the bus driver said. "That and a whole lot of other stuff, as I recall. But I thought there'd leastways be someone here to put you on the bus. Them's the rules, kids. No kids riding alone unless their folks put them on the bus and tell the driver where they're supposed to be let off."

Pixie was starting to shriek again when Dani interrupted. Reminding herself to be calm, she said, "But our mother can't come. She can't come to the bus stop."

"Yes," Pixie said more calmly, following Dani's example. Calmly—and pitifully. "She's too sick and we can't stay any longer because she's running out of food. If we stay any longer we won't have anything to eat."

"Is that right?" the bus driver said. "Well, that's a real sad story for sure. Real sad." He looked from Dani to Pixie and back again. Then he sighed, and started saying, "Well, now, maybe I could . . ." But he stopped in midsentence. Pushing past Dani, he said, "Come here, kid. Let me get a look at you." He was talking to Stormy.

Forgetting that he should stay back in the shadows while Dani and Pixie did the talking, Stormy had moved closer. Had moved into the light, and now was wincing and trying to pull away from the driver's hand on his shoulder. But the hand held on, and as he pulled Stormy forward into the light, the bus driver said, "Good Lord, kid. What happened to you? Who did this to you, son?"

But Stormy only shook his head and went on shaking it. Both Dani and Pixie started trying to answer but neither of their stories was going anywhere or making much sense. And anyway the bus driver had stopped listening. "You girls just be still a minute," he said. "I don't know what you're trying to pull, but it looks to me as how something's happened here that's not the kind of thing the bus company would want to get mixed up in. So why don't you kids go talk to someone here in town? Someone in charge, like the sheriff, maybe."

They tried, both Dani and Pixie tried to argue, but the bus passengers had started to straggle back across the street by then, and the driver turned his attention to them. At last Dani whispered, "Come on. Let's go. It's no use staying here."

"But where?" Pixie whispered frantically. "Where can we go?"

"I don't know," Dani said, and she didn't, but her feet seemed to be moving, taking her back into the deeper shadows. When they stopped she was back behind the Buick, and so were Pixie and Stormy. "Okay," Dani said, trying to sound calm and confident. "What we need to do now is—is to make a new plan."

"Okay," Stormy said, "a new plan."

Pixie nodded, but for once she didn't say anything. And, in

the next minute or two, neither did anyone else. But when a voice finally broke the silence it was Pixie's, and what she said was, "What about that truck idea?"

"What truck idea?" Dani asked. She knew what Pixie was talking about, of course, but she didn't feel like saying so.

"No. No truck." Stormy's voice was loud and clear. The clearest it had been all day.

"Why not?" Pixie asked him.

Stormy moved closer to Dani in the semidarkness. "Because," he said quickly and firmly, "because Dani says so."

Suddenly Dani was fighting a weird urge to do something she'd never done before or even wanted to do, and that was to reach out for Stormy and hug him. And she might really have done it, too, except she remembered just in time that a hug, even a small one, would probably hurt him a lot. So she just swallowed hard instead and said, "Yeah, I said no trucks, but . . ." She paused, thinking that stowing away on a truck might be their last chance. Stormy's last chance to get away from—from Rattler Springs. Of course, the odds weren't very good that, at that particular moment, the right kind of truck would be there in the yard. But then again . . .

"We'll look," she said. "We might as well go see what's here."

There were a lot of vehicles in Gus's parking lot that night, most of them parked near the garage, waiting, no doubt, for their turn over the grease pit. But out front, in the short-term parking area, there was only one truck. One van-type truck, closed and padlocked. So there was no hope there. But there was another parking area on the north side of the service station. And it had been there, Dani remembered, that she had seen the canvas-covered truck—and met the driver with the Gila monster face.

Clenching her teeth and shutting her mind to nightmare memories, she led the way behind the service station. As she picked her way past the door of Gus's famous rest room, and between piles of junk, mysteriously unrecognizable in the near darkness, she tried not to think about what had happened the last time she'd been there. But she couldn't help remembering how confidently she had climbed up on the box, and then . . . She was shaking her head, refusing to think about it, when suddenly a huge, shadowy shape loomed beside her. She tried to scream but her breath caught in her throat, and as she backed away she tripped and fell into a stack of old tires. She was still struggling to get to her feet when she heard Stormy's voice. She heard what he said, but there was another split second of terror before she understood.

What Stormy had said was, "Hi, Gus."

"Stormy?" Gus moved closer and switched on a flashlight. The beam moved from Dani's face to Pixie's and from there on to . . . "Stormy!" Gus said. "What in blazes happened to you?"

And then everyone was talking at once. Everyone, that is, except Stormy.

Gus was asking, "Was it that Grabler kid? Did he do this? I'll tan the hide off that . . ."

Pixie was saying, "And it's not just his face. You should see his back, and his legs."

And Dani was trying, without much luck, to make Gus

221

hear her whispered, "Gus. Gus. Don't ask him. I'll tell you what happened." It wasn't until she got hold of one of Gus's overall straps and jerked hard that he started paying attention. But once he started listening he quit asking questions.

The bus had gone by that time, had taken off on its belated trip to Reno, and the main street of Rattler Springs was very quiet. Inside his incredibly cluttered office Gus managed to uncover enough chairs for them all to sit down before he went back out to his electric ice chest and pulled out three root beers. He opened the root beers and passed them around, but after he'd watched Stormy for a minute, he pawed around among the bills and maps and newspapers on the counter until he found a box of drinking straws. Then he sat down and, turning to look at Dani, he said, "Awright, little lady. I want to hear what's going on here."

Dani gave him a long, cold stare before she said, "Well, what was going on was, we were running away. We were trying to get on the bus to Reno, only the driver wouldn't let us."

Gus nodded solemnly. "Awright, you were running away. All three of you?"

They nodded and Gus nodded back. "And why's that?" he asked, speaking directly to Dani. "Why'd you want to do a thing like that?"

Dani actually thought, None of your business. Even opened her mouth to say it. But somehow it didn't come out that way. She looked up into Gus's sad, droopy eyes under their shaggy eyebrows, and to her surprise she heard herself saying, "Because I need to get back home. Back to where I came from. I've been planning it for a long time. At first I was just going to go alone but then Stormy wanted to go too."

Gus looked at Stormy but he didn't ask him why he was running away. "Stormy's been part of the plan for a long time," Dani said. "You remember the lemonade stand? That was to get money for running away."

"I shorely do," Gus said. "And I recollect how Stormy here run off with your bankroll to save it from that Grabler kid." Dani couldn't help grinning a little, remembering Ronnie and the grease pit, and Gus chuckled too, showing his snaggly teeth and making his walrus mustaches bounce up and down. And even Stormy's swollen lips twitched a little.

But then Gus turned to Pixie and said, "So how 'bout you, little lady? Why were you fixing to fly the coop?"

So it was Pixie's turn. Dani leaned forward and stopped slurping up the last of her root beer. She couldn't begin to guess which story Pixie would tell Gus. Whether it would be the Frankenstein one or the forgotten kid one, or maybe something in between. But she felt sure that whatever it was it would be worth listening to. But then Pixie sat back, folded her hands in her lap—and proceeded to tell the truth, or something pretty much like it.

She told how her parents were scientists, not mad scientists or anything, but just people who loved studying and learning and making discoveries more than anything on earth, and how they'd always gone all over the earth to do it. "And then I guess I came along sort of by accident," she said, "but they took good care of me, at least they did when they remembered to. But sometimes they went where they couldn't take a little kid. Like on a glacier or in the middle of a desert. So they would leave me with my grandmother and most of the time that was okay with me. Only after a while I started wanting to go with them, and when I heard they were coming here, so close to home, I decided I was going to come too." She stopped and shrugged. "And so I did."

Gus nodded, his ugly old face puckered into a thoughtful frown. "And it warn't what you 'spected, I guess," he said.

Pixie shook her head. "No," she said. "No, it wasn't." And then to Dani's astonishment she began to cry. Pixie's crying was like everything else she did, different and dramatic and very impressive. For a moment Dani was really shocked. She put her arms around Pixie and patted her and tried to get her to stop, but for quite a while Pixie went on sobbing and wailing and thrashing around like a wounded wild animal. And then she stopped. Stopped wailing, sat up straight, wiped her eyes and looked up at Dani through soggy eyelashes. She didn't smile or anything, but in between the clumps of wet eyelashes Dani saw that weird flicker starting up again—or maybe it had been there all along.

"Awright," Gus said. "So what comes next? What are you kids going to do now that you've missed the bus?"

"I don't know," Dani said, "except that I better go home and tell my mother that we're all right. She's probably running all over town looking for us by now."

Gus shook his head. "Naw," he said. "Don't think so. Leastwise I saw your mom just a few minutes ago and she wasn't running around none."

"You saw my mother?" Dani couldn't imagine where. She

would have been at the store until around five-thirty or six and then she would have gone home and after that . . . For a while she'd have been home waiting but by now she'd surely be out looking for Dani. "Where was she?" Dani asked Gus. "Where did you see her?"

Gus grinned. "Right where she usually is," he said. "In the bookstore. I was walking up Main just a few minutes ago, and I saw as how the lights were still on in the bookstore so I sauntered by to take a look-see. And sure enough, there she was, along with Al Cooley and two or three other folk. Seemed to be some kind of a meeting going on."

"A meeting?" Dani said uneasily. She looked at Pixie and made her eyes say that didn't sound good. Leaning closer, she whispered, "With the sheriff, maybe. Maybe they've called the sheriff already."

"The sheriff?" Pixie sounded pleased. "Do you think it's the sheriff? Let's go see."

chapter

29

Stormy didn't want to go. When he heard Pixie say the sheriff might be at the bookshop he shook his head, and looked like he meant it. Dani knew why. He didn't want to have to answer questions about what had happened to him. Dani looked at Gus, asking him for help. "That's fine," Gus said. "You little gals go on down and see what's what, there at the store. Stormy and me'll just stay here." Then he lowered his voice and said, "Maybe I can get him down to the Careys and have Mabel take a look at him. See if there's anything she can do."

"Good idea," Dani whispered. Then she told Stormy he could stay with Gus and, grabbing Pixie's arm, pulled her out of the station.

"Mabel?" Pixie asked as they hurried down Main Street. "Who's Mabel?"

"Mabel Carey. An old lady who used to be a nurse," Dani said. "Closest thing to a doctor in Rattler Springs."

"Good," Pixie agreed. "He should see a doctor. Or the closest thing to one."

Gus was right, the bookstore's lights were still on, and from the dark street it was easy to see the people inside without being seen yourself. There were five people in the store. Linda was still there, Gus had been right about that, too. And her boss, old Al Cooley. And to Dani's surprise, Pixie's mom and dad were there too. But the fifth person was a stranger. An important-looking stranger in a suit and tie was sitting at Al's beat-up old desk, shuffling through a stack of papers. He was acting, Dani thought, kind of in charge, like a sheriff might be, but maybe a little too relaxed for a sheriff investigating a report of missing kids.

Dani and Pixie watched for a long time, peering in around the book displays in the window, but except for a lot of talking, nothing much seemed to be happening. As a matter of fact all the people in Al's bookstore were looking strangely relaxed, cheerful even, nodding and smiling and even laughing out loud now and then.

At one point Dani pulled Pixie away from the window and whispered, "That man at the desk. Do you think he's a sheriff?"

"Sheriff? No, that's just Mr. Bridgeman. He's a lawyer or something like that." Pixie sounded disappointed. "The sheriff must have left."

A few minutes later three men came out of Lefty's Bar and stood around talking. Talking and laughing and, it seemed to Dani, staring toward the bookstore. Pulling Pixie away from the window, Dani headed up the street. "Come on," she whispered. "Pretend we're just window-shopping." Pixie caught on right away, and they window-shopped all the way up the block and down the other side, until Main Street was empty again. But when they got back to the bookstore nothing had changed.

It was, Dani decided, as if nobody was the least bit worried, not even Linda. As if the Smithsons weren't the only parents around who could forget about their kid when there were other things to think about. Dani was beginning to feel really angry, watching them talking and laughing with the lawyer guy, while she and Pixie were still missing, at least as far as anybody knew. Lost on the desert, maybe, or even kidnapped.

A lot of time had passed and Dani had gotten a little careless about staying out of sight when Linda looked up at the clock and then out toward the window. Dani stepped back but it was too late. Her mother had seen her. "Come on," Dani said to Pixie, "we might as well go on in."

They might as well, she was thinking, face up to all the trouble they'd caused, and get it over with. But while Linda was unlocking the bookshop door she didn't look particularly troubled, or angry either, and all she did when Dani walked in was give her a quick hug and say, "Dani. I'm so glad you're here."

Pixie went over to talk to her parents and although Dani

couldn't quite make out what was being said, the discussion seemed to be calm enough. Actually, it looked like the most natural sort of parent-kid conversation Dani had ever seen them having.

It was then that Dani really began to feel resentful. It was as if the adults had all decided, for some sneaky psychological reason, to pretend that the whole thing was no big deal. That the whole running-away attempt had just been some unimportant little childish prank. Dani frowned and went on frowning while Linda introduced her to the man at the desk.

"Mr. Bridgeman, this is my daughter, Danielle," Linda was saying. And what Dani thought of saying was something like, "Yeah, I'm Dani. I'm the one who planned the whole thing and talked the other kids into going along with it. So if you have to put someone in jail, it might as well be me." But she had just gotten started when, from directly behind her, there was, not a knocking, but a thumping noise as if someone was banging on the bookshop's door with something besides their bare knuckles.

Everyone turned to stare, and sure enough, the person outside the door was Gus, and the reason he was knocking with his foot was because his arms were full of Stormy. A Stormy whose cuts and bruises were now accented by daubs of Mercurochrome, and who seemed to be sleeping peacefully in spite of all the thumping and jiggling. Dani ran to the door and the next few minutes were absolute confusion.

"Shhh," Gus was saying. "Let the little feller sleep. The pill Mabel gave him kind of knocked him out. Where can I put him? Anyplace he could sleep it off for a little while?" No one answered Gus's question right away because everyone, all the adults at least, were too busy making gasping sounds and asking Gus things like "My God, what happened?" And even though Dani would have been glad to explain no one was asking her any questions. When Al suggested that they could put Stormy to bed at his house, they all followed him out the back of the store and down the short path that led to his front door.

Dani had always liked Al Cooley's big, roomy old house. At the moment it was cluttered with half-full packing boxes, but the room where they put Stormy still looked pretty good. Besides a nice double bed, it had a bunch of other furniture, like dressers and chairs and even a small sofa. Dani sat down on the sofa and watched while Gus put Stormy on the bed and Al looked for a box of blankets. Stormy moaned once and then went on sleeping, and the whole crowd of people, Linda, Al, and Gus, the Smithsons and even Pixie and the lawyer, stood around staring at each other and down at Stormy's poor beat-up face. At last everyone tiptoed out. Everyone except Dani. Sitting down had been a mistake. She tried to get up but her muscles refused to cooperate. Suddenly she was too tired to move.

When her mother came back a minute later, Dani was curled up on the sofa and already half asleep. But she woke up long enough to say, "Someone ought to be here with him, in case he wakes up. And besides, I'm tired."

Her mother stared at her for a moment before she said,

"You do look exhausted. You stay right there." She found another blanket and as she was tucking it around Dani she whispered, "Dani, what *did* happen to Stormy? Do you know?"

Dani tried to nod but it was too much work. "Yes," she said. "Gus knows too. Gus can tell you."

"Yes, I suppose you're right," Linda said. "And Pixie. I'm sure Pixie can explain everything."

Dani was sure of that. For just a minute the thought of what a Pixie explanation might be like almost woke her up. But not for long. It couldn't have been more than a minute later that she fell fast asleep and stayed that way until early the next morning, when a faint sound made her open her eyes. Linda was standing beside Stormy's bed feeling his forehead with the tips of her fingers.

"Mom?" Dani said.

"Dani," her mother whispered. "You're awake. Can you get up now? I could use some help."

Feeling dazed and groggy, Dani struggled to stand up and, still wobbling a little, followed Linda down the hall to Al's kitchen. While her mother made oatmeal with brown sugar, and scrambled eggs and toast, Dani found the silverware and began to set the table. "Just three places," Linda said. "Al ate earlier and went off to the store."

Linda's first questions were about Stormy. "Did he sleep through the night all right?" she wanted to know, and then, "Dani, is it really true that it was Gloria who hurt him that way?" When Dani said it was true, Linda sighed and said that

231

Pixie had said so but they'd all found it hard to believe. "I guess we didn't want it to be true," she told Dani. "And you know how unbelievable some of Pixie's stories can be."

Dani said she knew.

Linda sighed again and went back to looking for things in Al's refrigerator, but the next time she turned around she was smiling in a way that Dani remembered but hadn't seen for a long time. "Dani," she said. "There is some good news. Some very good news. It seems that the land Chance left us is going to be quite valuable after all. The Smithsons located several important minerals on the property. Nothing as exciting as gold or silver, but something called fluorspar, for instance, that's used in the production of steel. Ivor and Emily asked Mr. Bridgeman to be here yesterday when they told me about it, to help explain things I needed to know. Mineral rights and things like that."

She stopped stirring the eggs for a moment and turned to look at Dani and her face had a shine about it. "Oh, Dani," she said, "it's so amazing. It seems that Chance's worthless old ranch is going to make us a very comfortable living after all. Which means . . ."

". . . we can move back to Sea Grove," Dani almost sang.

Her mother nodded. "Or anywhere else we might want to go."

For a moment they just stared at each other, with Dani holding a fistful of forks and knives and Linda still clutching her stirring spoon. They just stood there grinning for a while and then Linda's eyes narrowed angrily. Before she even said a word Dani guessed what they were going to talk about next.

So Dani helped her out by asking, "And the Grablers?"

Her mother sighed. "Oh, Dani. Those terrible people. What must have happened was that Mr. Grabler listened in on the conversations when Ivor was talking to his company on the hotel's phone. So he found out early on when the Smithsons began to make some interesting discoveries."

"Ooh," Dani said, "so that was why they wanted you to sell them the land in such a hurry? Before you had a chance to find out . . ."

"Exactly," her mother said.

They went on trying to get something done for several minutes but Dani, at least, was so angry at the Grablers and so excited about everything else that she couldn't remember what she was supposed to be doing. She was still staring at the same handful of forks and knives when Linda interrupted her dreams by saying, "Dani. Last night, while you were sleeping, Pixie told us some pretty amazing things. About the three of you running away?"

Uh-oh, Dani thought. Here it comes. Here it comes at last. "Yes," she said. "Yes, we really did. We started out anyway. We just didn't get very far."

Linda looked shocked and then bewildered. "But when? When did all this happen?"

"You mean you didn't even notice?" Dani was beginning to feel the way Pixie must feel—forgotten. As if her mother had forgotten to notice that her only kid had been missing for most of Thursday. Or at least from noon until way after dark. "Didn't you notice I wasn't home for dinner?" she asked accusingly.

Linda looked shocked. "No. No, I didn't because I wasn't there either. The Smithsons came into the shop during the afternoon and told me that they were expecting Mr. Bridgeman to arrive around dinnertime. And then they asked me if I could be at a dinner meeting." Linda shrugged and shook her head. "I couldn't imagine why, but I said all right. And then Ivor said he would bring some sandwiches over from the grill because it would be best if we could eat right here in the shop where it would be more private. So I said I could, but that I'd have to run home and let you know. Then Emily told me they'd left Portia with you, and she insisted on giving me enough money for you girls to eat at the grill. It must have been around five o'clock when I ran over to the house. You weren't there, of course, and now I know why, but at the time I thought you probably were downtown or out on the bicycle. So I just left a note and the money on the kitchen table."

"Oh." Dani was beginning to see what had happened. "By then we'd already been gone a long time. But the bicycle was there, though. Right there on the front porch. Didn't you see the Black Phantom?"

Linda shook her head. "I suppose it was there, but I used the back door."

It wasn't until then that it began to sink in, that no one had even known that they'd run away. It was an amazing thought. All that time while she and Stormy were nearly dying from sunstroke in the gully, and dodging rattlesnakes in the tunnel, and then being turned down by the bus driver, no one had even known that they were missing. But there was an important part of the story that her mother still didn't know. And that was . . .

"Mom," she said. "There's something else you ought to know. About why we ran away."

"Oh, I think I understand about that." Linda's smile looked a little sad. "I know how you felt about living in Rattler Springs, and how much you wanted to get back to Sea Grove."

"Yes," Dani agreed. "That's what it was for a long time, but the important part is, I changed my mind. I decided not to because . . ." She paused and then shrugged. She'd decide how to explain that later. When she went on she only said, "Even after Pixie got enough money for bus tickets I told her I wasn't going. I was even going to stop planning about it. That is, I was until . . ." She nodded toward the bedroom where Stormy was sleeping. "That's why," she said.

Linda sighed. "Yes, yes, I understand," she said. And just a second later she looked up and added, "Well, good morning, Stormy. How are you feeling?"

And there he was standing in the doorway. The swelling around his mouth had gone down just a little but his smile was still lopsided. "I'm hungry," he said.

Dani and Linda both smiled too. At Stormy first, and then at each other.

chapter
30

The O'Donnells never did go back to live in Jerky Joe's historic old cabin. In fact it was the very next day after the Great Runaway Adventure didn't quite happen that they began to move to another house. But not to Sea Grove. Sea Grove, it turned out, was still a few weeks away. A few weeks in which mining operations would be set up out at the ranch and then, after the results were measured, the O'Donnells would begin to collect their mineral rights income.

But in the meantime it was important for them to find someplace else to live as soon as possible. For instance, before Linda got around to telling the Grablers that she wasn't going to let them buy the ranch. And exactly why she wasn't! Which meant, of course, no more Jerky Joe's cabin. It was a problem that got solved in an interesting way.

It turned out that Al Cooley had never liked the Grablers much, and now that he was about to leave town he didn't mind saying so. And another thing he wouldn't mind was letting the O'Donnells use his house for a few weeks.

Al's house was old too. Not a lot newer than Jerky Joe's cabin maybe. But it had been built for one of the owners of the old silver mine, so it had been a better house to start with. There was a nice bathroom with tile on the floor and a real claw-foot bathtub. And, best of all, there were three bedrooms, so nobody had to sleep in the living room anymore. Linda shared Dani's bedroom until Al left, after which they would each have a bedroom of their own. Linda and Stormy thought the Cooley house was great, and even Dani had to admit that, for a Rattler Springs house, it wasn't all that bad.

So it was the day after the failed runaway attempt, and a few days before Al took off for Arizona, that the O'Donnells began to move into his house. Linda was going to go on working in the store until all the books were sold, and after that she had the job of finding a new renter for the store and, as soon as the O'Donnells didn't need it anymore, for the house as well.

Linda and Dani started moving their clothing and kitchen things that very first day. And on Wednesday, after Al had left for Arizona, Gus and a couple of his friends helped move the heavy stuff. By Thursday, when Linda went back to work in the bookstore, there was nothing left in Jerky Joe's cabin except a few boxes of odds and ends. Dani was about to cross Main Street carrying one last box when something awful happened. She ran into Ronnie Grabler.

It was a pretty touchy situation, but it might have been a lot worse except the Rattler Springs mail truck had just arrived, which meant that lots of people were downtown to get their mail. That made a difference because, while Ronnie certainly didn't mind hitting girls, he didn't like to do it when a bunch of people were watching. So Dani wasn't afraid to say what she felt like saying when Ronnie blocked her path and said, "We kicked you out, so now you're bumming off old Cooley. That right?"

What Dani said, loud and clear, so all the people standing in line outside the post office could hear, was, "We're moving out of your crummy cabin, if that's what you mean. And you might be interested to know that my mom is talking to a lawyer about how your dad tried to swindle her out of her property." Some of the people in the post office line laughed and a couple even clapped and cheered, and Dani marched around Ronnie and headed across the street.

Apparently it took a while for Ronnie to decide whether, under the circumstances, he could get away with slugging a girl, because she was halfway across Main Street before he caught up with her. This time he didn't try to stop her but he stomped along beside her long enough to say, "Well, you and your ma better watch out because Gloria knows where her kid is now, and is she mad! And everybody knows what happens when old Gorgeous Gloria gets mad."

This time Dani didn't even try to answer. Of course Gloria would know by now. Stormy hadn't been outside of the house since Gus carried him in, but in a town like Rattler Springs nobody could keep a secret for long.

In the bookstore Linda was talking to Mrs. Alwood, who'd come in to buy a book and probably to sneak out with a few more *True Romances*. Dani put down the box of knickknacks and stood around waiting impatiently for Linda's customer to leave. As soon as Mrs. Alwood finished snooping around the magazine rack, and then scooted out the door, Dani asked, "Where's Stormy?"

"He was in his room when I left. Why?" Linda looked worried. "I didn't like leaving him alone, but when I asked him to come to the store with me, he didn't want to. I think he's worried about seeing his mother."

"Yeah, I know," Dani said. "And I guess he ought to be. Ronnie just told me that Gloria knows where Stormy is and she's mad. Ronnie said she's really mad."

"She's mad?" Linda's face had an unfamiliar tightness around her mouth and eyes. "*She's* mad!" she said again, and, whirling around, she ran out of the shop with Dani right behind her. They found Stormy sitting on the floor of his room looking through a box of stuff that Al had left behind. Antique toys that used to belong to Al's kids, and things like that.

Stormy looked up quickly when they burst in. "Hi?" he said, making it into a question.

"Hi," Linda said. "Just checking. You all right?" Stormy said he was.

Back in the living room Linda told Dani that they shouldn't leave Stormy alone anymore. "Not till this custody question is settled."

"Custody question?" Dani asked.

"Yes." Linda put her hand on Dani's arm. "I've been talking to Mr. Bridgeman about the possibility of getting Stormy legally removed from his mother's custody."

"Well, good," Dani said, but then she began to put two and two together. "But then where would he live?" She began to get the answer before she'd even finished asking the question. "Ooh," she said. "I get it."

"And what do you think?" Linda asked.

Dani had to think about it. That would mean having Stormy around all the time, instead of just most of the time. And it would also mean all the hassle of having a younger brother when she'd always been an only child. It would be, she decided, a real pain in the neck. To have an extraordinarily stubborn, hardheaded nonreader for a younger brother! Who, on the other hand, was kind of brave. And loyal. Superloyal, actually. After a minute she shrugged. "Sure," she said. "Why not?"

But that very night, right after dinner, there was a loud knock on the front door and when Linda opened it there stood Gloria Arigotti. Dani and Stormy had been playing dominoes on the dining room table but as soon as he heard his mother's voice Stormy ran out of the room and down the hall to the bathroom. Dani heard him turn the lock on the bathroom door before she got up and crossed the living room to stand beside her mother.

Gloria's blond hair was wild and stringy, her face was streaked with tears and mascara and there was a whimpering sound to her voice. Tugging at the latched screen door, she said, "I've come for my kid. I want my kid back."

Linda's eyes had gone narrow and that unfamiliar stiffness was there again, around her mouth and chin. But her voice was calm as she said, "No, Gloria. You can't have him back. He doesn't want to go, and I won't let you have him."

Gloria's pitiful face disappeared in a flash and the one that took its place was hard-eyed, tight-lipped and pretty scary. But Linda went on talking quietly. "Listen, Gloria. I have all sorts of witnesses who will testify as to what you did to Stormy last week. People like Mabel Carey, who doctored his injuries. And Mr. Bridgeman, who's a lawyer, says that if we have to go to court you will lose. And you could lose not only Stormy, but your own freedom as well. Mr. Bridgeman says that you could very well wind up in prison."

"Prison?" Gloria's voice had gone high and screechy. "What the hell you talking about? For knocking my own kid around a little I could go to prison? Everybody knocks their kids around when they need it."

"No," Dani heard herself yelling, "you're lying. Good parents don't! Not ever!"

There was a moment's surprised silence. Gloria stared at Dani through the screen door for what seemed like a very long time before she turned around and staggered off down the path. They watched her go until she disappeared around the corner. Then Linda put her arm around Dani's shoulders and gave her a hug. "You all right?" she asked.

"I'm okay," Dani said, "but Stormy's locked in the bathroom."

Neither Dani nor Linda slept very well that night. At least Dani certainly didn't, and lying there awake, she kept hearing footsteps as Linda went down the hall to check on Stormy. Gloria didn't come back that night, however, and by the next afternoon everyone in town knew that she'd quit her job at the hotel, packed her bags and hitchhiked out of town. So that was that, except that Mr. Bridgeman was working on some papers that would make the O'Donnells Stormy's legal family.

Dani wasn't too sure how Stormy felt about his mother taking a powder, because he still didn't allow anyone to talk about her. But as far as she could tell he didn't seem to be too unhappy about becoming a permanent guest at the O'Donnells'. Which wasn't too surprising considering the fact that he'd been pretty close to permanent for quite a while. And it wasn't long before he began to behave normally again. Stormy normal, anyway, like eating everything in sight, begging Dani to read to him and drooling over the Black Phantom whenever Pixie brought it into town.

Pixie was still living at the ranch and visiting the O'Donnells every few days, but that probably wasn't going to last much longer. It seemed that she had decided to go back to live with her grandmother in San Francisco. But she would write, she told Dani. She would write to Dani and Stormy and after they'd moved she would come to visit. After all, San Francisco wasn't that far from Sea Grove.

Linda worried about Pixie sometimes. "I really like Ivor and Emily," she told Dani once, "but I'm afraid they just aren't cut out to be parents. They try to be, I think, but it just seems to be something that it's hard for them to keep their minds on."

But Dani told her not to worry about Pixie. "After all, she

242

gets along great with her grandmother. And I don't think she misses her parents that much. At least not very often."

"But you said she cried about them. You told me how hard she cried when she told Gus about her parents."

"Yeah," Dani said. "But I think that was mostly Pixie hysterics. I think people like Pixie really need to have something to be hysterical about now and then. Don't you?"

Linda laughed, and after a minute or two she said, "You know, I think you just may be right about that."

The next time Pixie came to visit she was being a little hysterical again, but this time it wasn't about her parents. This time she was all excited about the miners and engineers who were living at the ranch now, working on the mining project and staying in big air-conditioned house trailers. According to Pixie, miners and engineers seemed like normal people, at least right at first. But after a while they started doing weird things and it turned out that most of them were actually aliens from outer space. Martians, probably, who were using the antennas on top of their trailers to contact their home planet. Pixie got very excited about how dangerous it was to have Martians living in your backyard. It made a good story and Stormy seemed to enjoy it. But Dani was pretty sure he didn't believe it, at least not entirely.

There was another story that he liked even better, and that was the one where Pixie said she wouldn't be able to ride a bicycle when she was back in San Francisco, so when she left Rattler Springs she was going to leave the Black Phantom with Stormy. He really seemed to believe that one and Dani certainly hoped it would turn out to be the truth.

Up until the end of June, Linda kept promising they could leave for the coast by the end of July. She was expecting her first check from the mining company by then and she felt sure it would be enough to hire a van and some movers and pay the first month's rent on a house. But things always move more slowly than they're supposed to, and it was during the first week in July that Linda asked Dani if she'd be too disappointed if they put off moving until the end of August.

They'd been sitting on Al's big screened porch at the time, drinking root beer floats. At least Linda and Dani were still drinking theirs. Stormy had finished his and had started pounding the beanbag chair into shape, getting ready to settle down to listen to *Peter Pan*. "But I'm sure we can leave by then," Linda said. "I've been figuring very carefully, and I'm almost sure we'll be able to move by the end of August."

"The end of August." Dani slammed her glass down on the table.

"I know," Linda said. "I'm disappointed too, but . . ."

Dani got up and went out into the yard. It wasn't quite dark yet but the sun had set, and above the sleek black hills the endless desert sky was streaked and layered with weird shades of red. She stood there for a long time watching how the layers of color oozed and blended above the sharp-edged silhouette of the hills. It was, she had to admit, beautiful in a breathtaking sort of way. Cruel and deadly maybe, like she'd always thought, but certainly beautiful. And someday when she was back where she belonged, she might even admit it out loud. She might even tell people how gorgeous the desert could be. "Not yet," she told the silent sky, "but someday, maybe."

But in the meantime there were things that needed to be said to other people. She turned back toward the house, where Linda and Stormy were still sitting right where she'd left them when she slammed out through the screen door. Linda was looking sad again, and for just a second, Dani felt the way she used to—guilty and, at the same time, angry at Linda for making her feel that way. But then suddenly she found herself remembering how Linda had been that night when she'd told Gloria she couldn't have Stormy back. Dani was still thinking about that other Linda when she went back into the screen porch, sat down and said, "Well, I guess I can stand Rattler Springs for one more month."

"Yeah, me too," Stormy said. Then he gave the beanbag an especially fierce punch and muttered, "Come on, Dani. Aren't we ever going to read *Peter Pan?*"

"Sure we are." Dani settled back, opened the book to the first page and in a slightly sarcastic tone of voice said, "And then we're probably going to read every book in the Sea Grove library."

"Yeah." Stormy grinned. "And every book in the whole world."

"Sure, why not?" Dani said.